# Castaway in the Caribbean

by

**Janice Horton**

Copyright @ 2015 Janice Horton

The right of Janice Horton to be identified as the Author of this Work has been asserted by her in accordance with the Copyright, Designs and Patents Act 1988.

All characters and events in this publication, other than those clearly in the public domain, are fictitious and any resemblance to any actual institution, organisation, or person, living or dead, especially pirates, events or locales, is purely coincidental.

All Rights reserved. No part of this publication may be reproduced, stored in a retrieval system, or transmitted, in any form or by any means, without the prior written consent of the author.

Edited in British English

Kindle Reader Edition V20

**Romantic Adventure Fiction**
**by Janice Horton**

The Backpacking Bride
The Next Adventure
The Backpacking Housewife
Island in the Sun
Castaway in the Caribbean
Nola
Reaching for the Stars
Bagpipes and Bullshot
When We First Love

**Non Fiction**
How To Party Online

**For:**

Trav, my real-life romantic hero…

**What the readers say…**

'Who doesn't love an adventure? Especially when it's set in the Caribbean!' *Linn B Halton*

'Adventure, danger, romance… perfect for whiling away a lazy summer afternoon.' *BestChickLit.com*

'A fun adventure that's fast paced and mentions Treasure Island.' *Comet Babe's Books*

'A very entertaining fun read.' *The Book Maven*

'A lively romantic adventure, hugely entertaining, and enjoyable.' *Books4U*

'Who doesn't dream about a vacation in the Caribbean?' *R is for Reviews*

# Foreword by the Author

For the purposes of research, I was incredibly fortunate to spend a whole summer exploring many of the Caribbean islands and, despite my tendency for sea sickness, I also spent a lot of time in boats. I even got to sail around Tortola, the larger of the British Virgin Islands, in a restored schooner used in the filming of the original *Pirates of the Caribbean* movie.

The Virgin Islands inspired me with the modern day setting for *Castaway in the Caribbean* because, of this chain of around ninety small islands, islets, cays and rocks in the Caribbean Sea, many are uninhabited. But I eventually settled down to write this romantic adventure story on the Caribbean island of Utila, the smaller of the three Bay Islands, just off the coast of Honduras. Likened to the Key West of long ago, Utila is a quaint, unspoilt and laid-back little island. It sits on the largest barrier reef in the western hemisphere and so it's also a paradise for scuba diving, which is what my husband was doing every day, while I was writing. Research is a valuable tool for a writer, so I do hope all the fun and adventure I had in the Caribbean has found its way into the pages of *Castaway in the Caribbean*.

*Janice xx*

**Castaway in the Caribbean**

*Vacationing on the beautiful Caribbean island of Antigua, Janey Sinclair is persuaded by her magazine editor boss to do a quick island hop in order to supervise an impromptu photo-shoot for the front cover. With no flights immediately available, Janey is directed to the harbour.*

*Captain Travis Mathews hates tourists, although he's not above making a bit of money off a prissy and sharp-tongued young British girl when she's desperate to get to the neighbouring island of Tortola.*

*After striking a deal, they set off together in Travis's weather-beaten old boat. When the vessel comes to a sudden full stop in the sea, the mismatched pair end up as castaways on an uninhabited island.*

*In this fast moving romantic adventure about a vacation that turns into a tropical nightmare there's more fun than you'll find in any travel brochure.*

# Chapter One

Despite being wrapped up in her winter coat, Janey Sinclair was shivering as she marched over North Bridge in the direction of her office. It was freezing, so impossible for her not to reflect on this time last year, when she had been whisked away by her boyfriend to the tropical island of Antigua. It was a memory forever etched in her mind: hot sun, hot sand, even hotter boyfriend and, well... it had all been really *really* hot.

She sighed as she pushed her way through the heavy swing doors of the old building. Her steps echoed on the polished cold marble floor of the foyer as she followed the white lines of icy light that streamed in from the tall glass windows. She took the lift, and in the few moments that it took her to reach the top floor, she thought about Mark and how it had been a really *really* long week.

Then she stepped out into the bustling reception area of *Hot Scot Magazine*.

'Janey, you are just in time to help me choose our June cover!' Gwen, her editor, enthused. She held up two contenders. 'A highland landscape or a silhouetted castle ruin?'

Janey tried not to roll her eyes and began removing her coat and scarf. 'How about we go for something more contemporary?'

Behind her designer spectacles, Gwen looked intrigued. 'And by contemporary, you mean...?'

Janey tilted her chin and stared at a point just beyond Gwen's left shoulder. 'I see a beautiful Scottish girl standing on a beach in the Outer Hebrides. We should try to get Nola Nichols.'

Gwen's eyes lit up. 'Yes, of course. That's a fantastic idea. She's taking the modelling world by storm right now and she's from Glasgow. Oh, Janey, those came for you just a few minutes ago.' Gwen nodded in the direction of Janey's desk and to a bouquet of fresh flowers. 'And they must have cost him a fortune. I mean, who can afford sunflowers in February?'

Janey glanced at the card and smiled. *See you tonight at our place xxx*

She sighed dreamily. 'And he knows exactly how to bring a little sunshine into my life…'


'Their place' was a little restaurant off the Royal Mile. It served French food with a Scottish twist and it was here that she and Mark had first met, on a blind date set up by a well-meaning mutual friend. Since then, their relationship had grown into something steady and they'd made a point of meeting here every Friday night at eight pm as a preamble to their weekends together.

Mark King was a tall, dark, very handsome, and highly successful man who could afford to take her out to expensive restaurants like this one and to buy her out of season flowers. It was just a shame that they couldn't spend as much time together as she would have liked.

His heavy workload, his long hours, his busy court schedules, meant they only ever saw each other at weekends, and it sometimes felt to Janey like they were having an affair rather than a serious relationship.

'Darling Janey!' Mark sprang to his well-heeled feet as soon as she walked into the restaurant.

She rushed into his open arms, pressing her face against his shirt and crushing the sunflower she held in her hand. He was still wearing a formal suit, which told her that he hadn't yet had time to go back to his apartment and change into something that he considered more casual for the start of their weekend. She inhaled his signature cologne: a hint of woodnotes and old leather mixed with lime citrus. It smelled warm and sophisticated and expensive; so very him.

As they sat down opposite each other, the sommelier rushed over to pour their signature wine – a Chateauneuf-Du-Pape; *'a hint of sensuous sophistication mixed with zest'* according to Mark, who was a bit of a wine connoisseur. They'd enjoyed a bottle of this particular wine on their first date and then every Friday since. As a polite gesture, they were always offered a menu, but they always had the same meal. Mark had the Angus Steak, very rare, and Janey had the Chicken Balmoral with a whisky jus.

Some might have thought this quirky repetition rather boring, but Mark liked his routine and he particularly liked to recreate all moments he had enjoyed, so Janey was happy to go along with it.

It made him happy. She found it reassuring.

She always knew where she was with Mark.

'Oh look, I've squashed the flower you sent me.' she said sadly, holding up the drooping bloom.

He smiled. 'No matter. I sent you sunflowers as clue to the surprise I have for you. You have to guess what it is...'

'You have a surprise – for me?'

Last week, he'd given her a beautiful yellow gold necklace to match the bracelet he'd given her the week before. Was this the matching earrings, she wondered, a tad hopefully?

'Erm… now let me think…' she pondered, playing along with the game. 'Okay, then let me see… It's golden and its round…'

*Oh my goodness – it's a ring!*

Her heart swelled with excitement. She had dreamed of this moment; the moment that someone loved her so very much, that more than anything else, they wanted to be with her for the rest of their life.

*Should she accept straight away or tell him that she had to think about it? But really, what was there for her to think about? She was thirty years old and they had been together for three years. Okay, not three whole years, but three years of weekends. And then there was the one week holiday in Antigua last year. That all added up to over a year of sharing the same bed.*

'Like the sun!' she concluded, teasing him into thinking that she hadn't guessed.

'Yes. That's it! I've just booked for us to go back to *our* hotel in the Caribbean.'

He slid the holiday confirmation across the table towards her, and all thoughts of necklaces, bracelets and rings immediately disappeared when she realised she was escaping from the horrible cold Scottish winter and heading for tropical sunshine again.

*Oh what an adventure! Sun and sea and beaches and sand and hot sunshine!*

'You mean, the place we went to last year? We are going back to The Paradise Beach?'

'Of course – where else? We fly out on Monday morning.'

Janey was just about to shout for joy when she suddenly saw all the obstacles in her way.

'Monday? Oh no, I can't. You see, I'd have to ask Gwen for the time off. I still have holiday to take, but we still have to put the June issue to bed. She'd never give me the time off at such short notice.'

Mark smiled smugly and reached out to take her hand. 'Darling, it's all organised. I've already spoken with Gwen. She has granted you a week's leave. All you have to do now is pack your suitcase.'

They flew premium class, so while all the economy passengers were still queuing at the gate, they were whisked through and onto the aircraft to toast each other with foaming flutes of champagne. Once they were in the air, Mark, who didn't actually enjoy flying very much, popped a couple of anxiety pills into his mouth and fell promptly asleep. Janey happily stretched out in her fully reclining seat and finished off what remained of the champagne, while watching romantic comedies on her personal TV screen. In no time at all, or so it seemed, they were preparing to land in Antigua.

As the plane descended, she looked out of the window to see palm trees swaying on the white sand beaches of the coastline below and the sun shining on the blue Caribbean Sea. She turned in excitement to Mark, who was still sprawled out beside her.

'Wake up, darling. Look, we are here!'


That same afternoon they were relaxing on their beach loungers, sipping cocktails, as Janey happily took in the scene around them: the five star resort, the pristine white sand, the warm clear lapping waters of the Caribbean Sea. 'Oh, to think only yesterday we were freezing in Scotland and today we are melting in the Caribbean.'

'You certainly look hot,' Mark told her, his voice deep and deliberately playful.

Through her designer sunshades, she watched the sexy smile playing on his lips and allowed her gaze to wander over his naked torso. This was a very different

Mark. This wasn't Barrister Mark. This was Holiday Mark who might be up for a few adventures in and out of the bedroom. It might seem like she'd not seen this version of him since last year, but she had to make allowances for that, as back home he was Very Successful Mark who had a Very Important Career.

He also had a very attractive body. He was long and lean and he looked after himself. He watched what he ate. He worked out in a gym every morning before work. He was meticulous.

'How about we go back to our room and cool down in the shower?' she suggested.

Giggling like naughty teenagers with their libidos fuelled with cocktails, taking a shower and going to bed in the late afternoon sounded like such a bold idea. Until they actually reached the bed. No sooner had their jet-lagged heads hit the soft pillows and their over-heated bodies grazed the cool sheets, than they both fell fast asleep.

The room was confusingly dark when Mark leapt from the bed to check the time on his phone. 'Have we missed dinner?'

Janey, still enjoying the feeling of being wrapped in drowsy luxury and the finest cotton sheets, urged him to come back to bed. 'I'm not hungry. Come back to bed, sweetheart?'

'No. Come on sleepy head. We have a reservation for eight pm.' He slapped her backside through the sheet. 'We can still make it if we get a move on.'

Strings of fairy lights and low-slung lamps led the way from their villa through a sandy avenue of palm trees to the hotel's open-air restaurant. Along the way, tropical frogs croaked and fireflies hovered and the air was heavy and warm.

Inside, at each table, a candle flame flickered in a glass lantern. A tropical sea breeze and overhead fans in the palm-thatched roof provided the air conditioning. The atmosphere was sultry. Glamorous loved up couples sat at the tables, either eating delicious looking food or holding hands. A reggae band was playing a familiar beat, and the sounds and smells of the Caribbean filtered towards Janey and Mark as they entered the restaurant with their fingers entwined.

They were met by the Maitre'd, who immediately recognised them from last year.

'Mr King and Miss Sinclair, welcome back to Antigua. Your table is ready. Please follow me.'

They were led to a reserved table. Janey recalled that it was exactly the same table they'd had last year.

Mark looked entirely satisfied. He tipped the waiter generously and ordered champagne. Then before they were even seated, he turned to Janey. 'Would you care to dance, Ms Sinclair?'

She smiled at him, bemused by the total accuracy of his re-enactment of the previous year.

On the dance floor Mark swept her into his arms. She closed her eyes and took in the scent of him, expecting a warm waft of the new cologne she had bought for him at the duty free, which she now realised had been an expensive mistake as he'd chosen to keep to his signature scent after all. They swayed together to the pulsing beat. The singer, a black man with long dreadlocks and a quirky-looking Rasta hat on his head, gyrated his snaky hips and shook a tambourine as he sang *'Could This Be Love'*. It was all so perfect and yet, also a bit surreal in its familiarity.

It was as if time itself had been caught in a loop, because here they were again, one year later, dancing to the same tune.

Only when the music changed tempo, did Mark lead her back to their table.

As they sat down, he continued to hold her hand and looked intensely into her eyes.

'Janey, there's something I want to ask you.' He spoke softly, his voice almost a whisper.

Locked in his gaze and loved up on music and afternoon cocktails, she waited quietly to hear what it was he was going to ask her.

'I'd planned to do this later, perhaps on the beach under the stars or something, but I simply can't wait any longer.'

Then he fumbled in his pocket and pulled out a small velvet box which he flipped open and slid towards her. Inside was not just one but two rings: a diamond solitaire and an etched gold band.

'Darling Janey, will you marry me?'

# Chapter Two

The next morning, after a sumptuous Caribbean breakfast, they were lounging around the pool with the whole day ahead of them in which to do nothing but relax. Janey had just applied a large squirt of sunscreen to her hands when her mobile phone rang from inside her beach bag. Mark groaned disapprovingly.

'Oh, Janey, I can't believe you have brought your phone, here of all places?'

She looked a little guilty. 'Habit, I guess. I'll just let it forward to my answerphone.'

But once she was sun-protected, she rummaged through her beach bag to sneak a peek at who had called her. It was Gwen. And she knew there was no way her boss would have called her while she was on holiday if it wasn't something super important.

'I'm sorry, darling, it's Gwen. I'm going to have to call her back.'

Mark scowled. 'How can you? When we promised each other that this time would just be us, for one week, without any distractions?'

Janey stood, wrapped her sarong around her waist. 'Well, then how about I go and get us another rum punch each?'

She made the call, worrying what might be happening back in Edinburgh.

'Gwen, I just saw a missed call from you. What's the matter?'

'Oh, Janey, I'm sorry. I know you are on holiday but our cover girl for the June issue, Nola Nichols, has been delayed out in the Caribbean at her shoot for *Vanity Flair* and her calendar is so tight that her agent wants to cancel out. But, you see, by flying over to Tortola and organising a quick shoot for us and then flying back again to continue your holiday you could salvage the whole situation. It will take you just a few hours at the very most.'

Janey could hardly believe what she was hearing. 'Gwen, we may be geographically close, but how can this possibly work when Nola was supposed to be on a Scottish beach for our June cover? I mean, how can Tortola look anything like the Isle of Mull?'

'Janey, with a bit of sunshine, the white sand bay at Mull can look exactly like a Caribbean beach, but if you prefer... have Nola pose in front of a green screen so we can drop the background in later. Darling, all you have to do is turn up in Tortola and get our cover shot before twelve noon tomorrow.'

'But, Gwen, you really don't understand. Mark asked me to marry him last night.'

There were squeals of excitement down the line which was followed by a brief silence while Gwen recalculated her strategy. Then she was back. 'Darling, you may not thank me now, but I'm sure you will later, when Mark realises that you have a career just as important as his.'

Janey had to bite her tongue. She only wrote about clothes and shiny baubles while every day Mark was in court practically saving people's lives. What she did didn't even come close to that.

'Gwen, Mark knows how much I love my job and my being an independent woman is, I'm sure, just one of the reasons he loves me.'

There was another pause while Janey felt sure Gwen was re-living that moment when Mark, invited to one of their recent in-house media events, bellowed something about *Hot Scot Magazine* being 'nothing more than silly entertainment' absolutely loud enough for all of their sponsors to hear.

'Oh, Janey, then please do this. If not for me then for the magazine. It's the June issue, after all?

Janey rolled her eyes in frustration, knowing there was simply no way out of this situation. It actually did make perfect sense for her to pop over to Tortola, if that's where Nola Nichols was right now. Then she cursed herself for having had the alternative magazine cover idea in the first place because, if she hadn't opened her big mouth, Gwen would have been perfectly happy with the usual castles and landscapes.

'Oh, okay. I'll do it.'


Mark was not at all happy. 'I think this is an unreasonable request and a terrible invasion of our privacy. We are on holiday, we are engaged to be married, and our time here is precious. We ought to be spending it together, not apart. And besides, I've arranged for us to do a tour of Nelson's Dockyard this afternoon.'

'But we did Nelson's Dockyard last year, darling. Why don't we make some new memories this time? Why don't you come to Tortola with me this afternoon instead?' she pleaded.

He crossed his arms over his chest, lowered his head and began to sulk.

Janey wondered if he did that in the courtroom when things weren't going his way.

'It could be fun, Mark. Think of it as an adventure. You do know that Tortola is where they filmed the first *Pirates of the Caribbean* movie, don't you?'

Mark almost gave himself whiplash as his head snapped up. 'Really?'

*Pirates* was one of his favourite movies and one they'd watched together many, many times, over and over and over.

'Yes. You could take a tour around the set of Port Royal while I'm working.'

He sighed, shrugged, but then he agreed to come along after all.


'Excuse me, but can you help?' Janey asked the hotel's concierge, who was smiling at them from behind a small desk in the reception foyer. 'We need to get to Tortola later today. Can you please organise a flight?'

Only, rather than the enthusiastic response she was expecting, she was met with a look of sympathy.

'I'm so sorry, Miss Sinclair. The flight to Road Town, Tortola, departs from Antigua only in the morning.'

Janey looked to Mark, who had been staring sourly at a picture of a small plane on the Island Air advertising poster and was now looking rather relieved to hear that they couldn't leave straight away.

She turned to the concierge once more. 'Okay, then we'll take the morning flight instead. What time do we leave?' She handed over her credit card but the response was once again one of sympathy.

'I'm sorry, Miss Sinclair, but tomorrow's flight is cancelled due to it bein' a public holiday an' all.'

'So you are saying there are no flights today or tomorrow?'

'That's right. Not 'til the day after tomorrow.'

'But that will be too late. I'm supposed to be on Tortola tomorrow morning. It's important.'

'Then you should take a boat, Miss Sinclair. We can recommend a charter, if you'd like?'

Janey was immediately grateful for a solution.

'Yes, thank you. We'll do that. We'll take a boat.'

Mark, who had until that moment been sporting a pink-tinged slightly sunburnt face, suddenly looked decidedly pale. 'Oh no, Janey. No. No way!'

She turned to him in astonishment. *Hadn't he been listening? Taking a boat was the only way to get to Tortola in time to meet up with the photo shoot team and her star model?*

'What do you mean, Mark?'

He took her aside by the arm and lowered his voice so that only she could hear him. 'I don't do boats. I'm afraid I simply don't have the sea-legs for it. It's a family thing, an affliction, passed down through many generations of Kings.'

Janey's heart went out to him. He couldn't swim and he was afraid. 'Oh, darling, you don't need to be able to swim to go out on a boat. I mean, we flew here on an aeroplane, but we can't actually fly ourselves, can we?'

'Janey!' he snapped, clearly getting annoyed at her insistence. 'You simply don't understand. You'll just have to go without me and I'll wait here for you until you get back.'


At the marina, Janey followed the directions given to her by the hotel concierge that would lead her to a mooring post for *The Mermaid*; the charter boat personally recommended by Leo, the hotel manager. 'The boat's captain, Travis Mathews, is an old friend,' he had said. 'Mention my name and he'll not only take care of you but he'll give you a discounted price.'

Now, standing on the boardwalk at the dockside, looking at the shabby and paint-stripped hull of *The*

15

*Mermaid*, Janey was convinced that this couldn't possibly be the right boat. It didn't look capable of making its way out of the bay, never mind across the sea. Thinking that she must have made a wrong turn somewhere, while admiring some of the more luxuriously appointed yachts, she looked about and then checked her directions again.

'Miss Sinclair?' a male voice asked. It came from somewhere inside the boat.

'Yes. Yes I am. Where are you?' She peered over the rim of her designer sunglasses.

'I'm here.' The man's head suddenly popped up from below deck. 'Travis Mathews at your service.'

Travis climbed out of a hatch and stood upright. He was wearing a pair of dirty and torn overalls and he was smiling broadly at her. He wiped his oily hands on a rag before jumping onto the dockside to shake her hand.

Janey, dressed in a pale lemon coloured silk shift dress with matching wide brimmed hat, looked at him with distain and pointedly ignored his still grubby outstretched hand. 'Ah, good, then you were expecting me?'

'Yeah. Leo called to say you were coming over. He told me that you need a ride to Tortola.'

She laughed nervously and shrugged. 'Yes, but not in *this* boat, surely?'

He studied her for a moment and then he laughed loudly, as if she'd just told a very funny joke.

She noted his perfect teeth, dazzling white in the sharp sunlight; so typically American, she thought. Travis Mathews had short, curly dirty-blond hair, a very deep tan and a slow drawl to his deep-south accent. It was just a shame that his phoney smile didn't quite reach the corners of his incredibly blue eyes.

'We may be a little weathered but we are still seaworthy,' he assured her, as he reached into his pocket to pull out a pair of sunshades, which he slid quickly onto his face before he began to peel off his dirty overalls right in front of her, working them down over his torso and then hopping from foot to foot as he pulled them from each of his legs.

Janey desperately wanted to avert her eyes, but found that from behind the safety of her own sunshades, curiosity got the better of her when faced with his bare mahogany-tanned and muscled physique. 'But I saw you were just down in that hole fixing it. So it's obviously broken.'

He shook his head. 'No, no. I was down in the engine room *maintaining* her.'

'Well, I still think there has been a mistake. I can't possibly go out in this boat. I mean, it's too small for one and look...' She waved a polished finger at a machine that was spitting water out onto the deck. 'It's leaking!'

Travis's patience was clearly starting to thin as her criticism of his boat continued.

'Look here, lady, I'll have you know that *The Mermaid* is the best dammed boat in this dockyard.

And besides, you won't get another ride to Tortola today or tomorrow, not on a public holiday.' He crossed his arms over his bare chest. Janey couldn't help but note how strong they looked.

'On the contrary, I saw a yacht for hire just along the quayside there.'

Travis gave out a hoot. 'Then I hope you have your Skipper's Licence with you, lady, because you can't hire one those big fancy boats without one.'

At that moment, a darkly tanned and voluptuous-looking girl appeared from the same hole on deck that Travis had climbed out from. She wore a small string bikini top and thong-style briefs, which left nothing to the imagination.

Janey immediately supposed this was whom Travis had claimed to be *maintaining* below deck.

'Hey, Honey!' he called out. 'Would you go over to the fuel depot and let Booty Bill know that I'll need a couple more cans of fuel for tonight. I have to go to Tortola. You wanna come too?'

The girl shook out her long hair and spoke to him in a sexy mix of English and Latino.

'Lo siento perdon, Travis, I have a show tonight.'

Travis turned back to Janey. 'Honey dances for the tourists a couple of nights a week.'

The way he said 'the tourists' spoke volumes. This man clearly saw her and all other visitors to this island as nothing but a nuisance, except for when they were being useful to him as cash machines. Her response was heavily laced with sarcasm as they both watched Honey strut her shapely stuff down the boardwalk.

'Okay. How much will you charge me?' she asked him directly.

'Five hundred bucks,' he answered without any hesitation.

'Just so you know, I was promised a discount by your friend Leo.'

'That *is* with a discount.'

Janey's mouth dropped open in shock. 'You've got to be joking me, because a flight over to Tortola would cost me half that much!'

He shrugged and then casually reminded her that there were no flights to Tortola.

Reluctantly, she handed over the extortionate fare, while feeling increasingly annoyed with him for taking advantage of her situation. Gentlemen, she decided, didn't do that to a woman, and clearly Travis Mathews was no gentleman. She watched him fold the notes she'd given him and stuff them into his back pocket. 'Aren't you even going to count it?'

'No. I'll trust you. Here, let me take your bag and show you to your erm… cabin.'

Janey gripped her Hermes tote bag closer to her chest. In it she had a change of clothes and underwear and a few essential toiletries. It also contained some of Mark's anxiety tablets, which he had said would help her with any seasickness. She had never actually been in a boat before, except a rowing boat on Loch

Lomond one time, and so she had accepted them just in case she felt nauseous. 'No, thank you. I'll keep it with me. I think it probably cost me a lot more than you paid for this boat.'

# Chapter Three

Travis Mathews had looked up from below deck to see a vision of loveliness on his dockside. This vision had shoulder length blonde hair under her wide-brimmed hat and she had the body of a sea-nymph: long slim legs, a slim firm body, a pair of small round but perfectly formed breasts and a pert little behind. Luckily for him, he could admire this woman in her entirety, thanks to the sheerness of her pale yellow dress and the bright sunlight shining from directly behind her.

He'd called out her name and greeted her with his widest of smiles, as this particular punter at least had the good looks to go with the big bucks.

Then she'd peered over her sunglasses at him with those big icy green eyes of hers and he'd got the full benefit of her distaste. She said that she didn't like the look of his boat. Then she'd insulted his engineering skills. Then she'd glared at his girlfriend as if she were some kind of bimbo when Honey had more skills than most people gave her credit. Then there was all the bartering over the fare, very unlady-like in his opinion, which became an issue only because she'd made it one.

*Bloody tourists… they were all the bloody same.*

As *The Mermaid* sailed away from English Harbour, Janey sat on a hard wooden seat just behind the wheel house, which contained the steering wheel and control panel. She was wearing a large and dirty life vest. Travis Mathews had placed the vest over her head without any warning when she had stepped aboard, which immediately resulted in an oily smudge down the front of what had been a very expensive dress.

'Is this really necessary?' she had asked him, noting that he wasn't wearing one of these smelly rubber garments himself.

'Only if we sink,' he had responded cheerfully.

She had winced, but Travis had just kept on smiling at her through his straight white teeth.

'And how long exactly will it take us to reach Tortola?' she'd asked, also noting it was just after four o'clock in the afternoon by her watch.

'If we keep our speed to around twenty-five knots, we'll be there around ten pm.'

'Good. That suits me fine. I have an appointment at eight tomorrow morning.'

A short time later, as the Antigua coast line evaporated in their wake and the sun dipped towards the unbroken line of the horizon, Janey's mood softened. It was impossible not to appreciate the warm evening and the light breeze as they slipped across the calm sea, and even when they did encounter the occasional wave, the gentle rearing of the boat, the slap of water against the hull and the spray of fine mist on her skin, it felt exciting.

It was an adventure.

With her face tilted into the wind, Janey realised she was actually enjoying herself, and after a while she began to relax, gaining in confidence a little as the movement of the boat became more familiar to her. She even leaned over the side, to see white-tipped waves rolling against the sides of *The Mermaid* as it gathered speed.

To think, just a few days ago, she had been in freezing cold Scotland wishing to be somewhere just like this. This was a dream come true. She wasn't normally the adventurous type, well… she dreamt of adventures and she read about adventures, but she didn't normally live them like some people did. But right at that moment, she felt as if she was on an exciting journey. It was just a shame that Mark wasn't here to share it with her.

'Once we get to Tortola, you are welcome to stay on board until it's time for your morning appointment,' Travis told her from the wheel house and over the sound of the boat's engine. 'There's a bunk you can take below deck.'

'And is that in with my five hundred bucks or do I have to pay extra for that?' she quipped.

She was still stinging at the price he was charging her for this journey. If she'd been flying, she'd have at least been offered a complimentary drink by now.

He growled that it was indeed 'an all-inclusive' price and a 'very special offer'.

He put so much emphasis on the latter that Janey suspected he might be offering her something inappropriate so, just to be clear, she retorted that she didn't want or need any of his special offers.

'No, thank you. My editor has booked me into a hotel, so I won't need your bunk.'

Travis continued to growl. 'Okay, lady. Suit yourself.'

After an hour or so of relative silence between them, Travis stopped the boat and weighed anchor.

Janey stiffened in her seat. *What on earth was he stopping for?*

'This is about the half-way mark, so we'll stop and take a break. I have some sandwiches and snacks and drinks for us in there.' He pointed to a cool box on the deck. 'Besides, this is by far the best spot in the Caribbean to watch the sun go down. You can see all the BVIs from here.'

'The BVIs?' she queried.

'Yeah, the British Virgin Islands. Only eight of the islands are truly inhabited. The rest are just waiting to be explored. See right over there?' Travis pointed towards the last point of land amongst the misty chain of islands, islets and rocks.

The view was totally breathtaking. The sea was calm and there was hardly a ripple on the water or a breath of wind in the air. In her view was island after island, some bigger than others and others no more than a rock. Then there was the one far away in the misty muted distance that Travis was pointing out to her.

'Yes... yes, I do.'

'That's Norman Island. The inspiration for the book *Treasure Island*. Have you read it?'

'Yes, I have!' Janey confessed. 'It's my favourite book of all time.'

Travis frowned. 'Then you'll know that these islands have a hard history. In the old times of piracy, Blackbeard marooned his mutinying buccaneers on one of these islands with nothing but a bottle of rum. They all died slowly, one by one, in an agony of thirst and starvation. The poor souls.'

Janey looked horrified. Travis looked pleased.

She looked around them and took in the sheer remoteness of their position. Then she pointed over to the island that was closest to them. It was in shadow and undulating, with two equally high and rounded mountain peaks that looked exactly like the shape of a woman's breasts, complete with nipple peaks. Annoyingly, she was once again reminded of the magnificent curves on the girl who had climbed out of Travis's cabin below deck.

'And what about this one? What's this island called?'

'I call it Tit Island, because it looks like a big pair of tits,' Travis said, laughing heartily.

Janey felt herself blushing furiously. Travis Mathews was clearly one of *those* kind of men; the stereotypical kind who liked women with big breasts and bums and absolutely no brains. She turned away from him in disgust and stared ahead to where the big golden sun had now dipped below the horizon. She hadn't anticipated them stopping, but she reluctantly supposed that he had to eat his dinner. She accepted a beer from him but refused the food.

'Are you sure?' he said, shaking a sandwich under her nose. 'It's tuna. I made it myself.'

She held her breath and shook her head.

'Suit yourself, lady. All the more for me.'

She noticed him in the glow of lamp-light, studying her for a few minutes while he finished unwrapping his meal. She felt uncomfortable. *What was he thinking? Was he eyeing her up? Did he think she was attractive?* She licked her lips nervously as he continued to stare.

'What?' she eventually snapped.

'You really should eat something. I mean, if you don't mind me saying, you look like you could do with feeding up a bit.'

Janey glared at him. 'Actually, I *do* mind you saying that. It is so rude of you!'

'Well, it's rude of you not to eat my food,' he retaliated.

She turned her back on him while he ate. He chewed far too enthusiastically, in her opinion.

'Mmmm... there's nothing wrong with these sandwiches,' he told her, with his mouth full of bread and tuna.

'And there is nothing wrong with me being slim!' she retorted, her lips quivering in rage.

After a few minutes of angry silence, he was talking to her again. 'Leo told me you're a journalist. So what newspaper do you work for over there in the UK?'

Insulted at the idea of him thinking she was a media journalist, she felt she had to put him right.

'I don't work for a newspaper. I work for a magazine. And I'm based in Edinburgh.' Janey delved into her bag to bring out the latest issue and prove her point. She offered it to him.

He leaned forward to take it. 'Well, I can't say I've ever heard of this one.'

'Well, that's because it's a lifestyle and fashion magazine and you might be more of a *Ship Wreck Monthly* kind of guy.'

He laughed and then read aloud from the front cover: 'Ten ways to brighten your life with mirrors. Really?'

Janey rolled her eyes. 'Yes, really.'

'Well, here you don't need mirrors to brighten your life, lady. You need sunshades to lessen the glare.'

'Actually, my name is Janey. So if you don't mind, you can stop calling me "lady".'

Travis extended his hand once more. 'It's nice to meet you, Janey.'

This time she allowed him to fold his hand around hers. It felt warm and strong, slightly rough, probably from working with ropes and old boat engines.

He smiled at her and she smiled back and in that moment she couldn't help but to notice how his blue eyes crinkled at the corners in the most attractive way. When he finally released her hand, with his voice soft and drawling he said her name.

'Janey...?' The sound of it from his lips sounded so different.

'Yes...?'

'You really should try smiling more often. It suits you.'

Shocked by his bluntness, she snatched back her magazine.

He laughed. 'Look, I think you and I may have got off on the wrong foot.'

'Ha, you think?' She laughed too, but she certainly wasn't amused.

'Yes, I do. I think we should start over. How about we both make an effort this time?'

She looked at him with her chin raised warily. 'You want me to pretend that I'm not a tourist and that you're not a grumpy old sea captain?'

He raised his chin too. 'Yeah, why not? I'll try to be less judgmental if you stop behaving like a stuck-up little princess?'

She took a sharp intake of breath. *What was she thinking? This man was impossible.*

She checked her watch. 'You said our arrival time in Tortola is around ten?'

'Yep. That's about right,' he replied, ramming the last bit of his sandwich into his mouth.

Janey stood and steadied herself against the sway of the boat.

'Well, until then, I'll be in my cabin. Goodnight Captain Mathews.'

Below deck was tidier than Janey had expected but much smaller than she imagined. In fact, it was a little claustrophobic, but there was no way she wanted to spend another minute on deck in that awful man's company. There was a tiny kitchen area and then a small cabin beyond it with a bunk that was slightly bigger than a single bed but much smaller than a double size. There was a shelf full of books including, she noticed, *Treasure Island*, and a desk with a lamp on it and a wooden box. The box was quite beautiful with its macramé lid. Her fingers hovered over it as she wondered what was inside. It didn't have a lock on it, just a small catch. Curiously, she lifted the lid and saw there was a man's watch and some photographs of an older couple that she assumed must be his parents. Oh, and a couple of wedding rings. She thought about that for a moment before closing the lid quietly.

Next, she opened a cupboard door, looking for the washroom and found what she assumed must be Travis's wardrobe. In it hung three shirts and one pair of denim jeans. On a shelf there was a pile of unfolded t-shirts. She considered for a moment Mark's vast walk-in wardrobe, filled with his tailored shirts, his designer suits and his chosen brand of leisure wear, and then she reprimanded herself. It hardly seemed fair to compare Mark's lifestyle with Travis's, when he obviously had so little in comparison.

She opened a second door and peered inside. She found a toilet and a sink but no shower. What on earth did he do for a wash, she wondered.

*Maybe he just jumped overboard?*

She used the toilet and then to her anguish, discovered that water for flushing and operating the tap had to be accessed using a pump-style lever on the floor that didn't work too well.

Finally, she lay on the bunk for a few minutes, feeling the sway of the boat and feeling increasingly nauseous. If they still had another three hours before they reached Tortola, she might feel better if she slept and if she took a couple of Mark's pills.

*And maybe instead of two pills, she should take three?*

# Chapter Four

On Antigua, as the sun went down, Mark came in from the beach and showered. He dressed in lightweight linen slacks and a short-sleeved collared shirt, while considering how lonely it felt to be here without Janey, and even more so to sit alone at their table tonight for dinner.

He was welcomed into the restaurant by the ever attentive Maitre'd. He chose a bottle of his favourite wine and he glanced at the menu. On the second night here this time last year, he recalled having seared snapper and it had been delicious.

He looked around him at the couples surrounding his table and felt another pang of loneliness, this time tinged with a little vexation. He still thought that Janey had been entirely unreasonable in putting her work before him, especially when they had just got engaged. Perhaps when they were married he could talk her into working part-time, until he got her pregnant, which he intended to do as soon as possible, as she wasn't getting any younger after all, and then she could give up working for that silly rag and raise his children. He'd finally agreed with his mother that now was about time he settled down and raised a family.

Casting his eyes back to the menu, he was annoyed to see there was a Caribbean-themed evening planned. The hotel certainly hadn't done anything like that last year. He sighed unhappily.

It seemed this holiday was full of surprises and not all of them were good ones.

When the steel band on the stage struck up with a heavy drum beat, six brightly dressed and barefoot girls danced onto it in flowery costumes. They also wore flowers in their hair and leafy vines on their arms and legs. They swirled and twirled in front of the band and then spilled out onto the dance floor, swaying and stamping their feet to the music beat, which had now filled the air.

Everyone in the audience stopped eating or chatting to watch the show and at that moment the room dimmed as another girl came out onto the stage. The spotlight fell onto her as she danced, cavorting her body slowly and purposefully, rolling her hips to a single and almost hypnotic drum beat. Like all the other girls, she was barefoot and her legs and arms where entwined with flowers on twisted vines. She held her hands together as if they were bound high above her head, on which she wore an enormous flower festooned headdress. Her hips swayed and her stomach undulated, and Mark's mouth dropped open as he watched her move. The girl had an incredible body.

She moved slowly to the centre of the stage. Underneath all the flowers, she was wearing a very small bra-style top, so small it could hardly contain her large round breasts. She also wore a skirt, so short that Mark could clearly see her firm smooth buttocks as she flicked her hips from side to side. Her eyes were low and her lips full and pouting as she locked her dark sultry eyes onto the only man sitting alone in the restaurant. She danced towards him, and as much as Mark wanted to look away, he found that he couldn't.

Janey woke to hot sunlight streaming onto her face from a small porthole. It was morning; they must have reached Tortola while she slept. Travis must have left her sleeping despite her telling him she had a hotel reservation. Then she remembered taking Mark's pills and realised it was entirely possible she had been unconscious rather than sleeping. Her dry mouth and sore head was testament to that theory. She staggered up the ladder to the deck.

Seeing Travis sitting on the deck, she begged him, 'Do you have any tea?'

While she waited for his response, she squinted against the painful shards of light bouncing off the water surrounding them and noted that he had all sorts of bits and pieces around him; small wires and things.

'What's going on? What's happened?'

It was then she noticed that Tit Island was exactly where it had been last night.

'We have a situation here,' Travis told her.

Her voice came out in a shriek of panic. 'Is it the boat? Is it broken? Can you fix it? And what the hell time is it, anyway?'

She checked her watch. It was seven thirty in the morning.

*Oh my goodness… Nola Nichols would be at the photo shoot in half an hour!*

Travis continued to mutter into his small wires. 'No, it's not the boat. It's the radio. I've just done an operational check for a drop in voltage and now I'm just going to perform a reception test.'

'Oh, for heaven's sake, can't you mess around with that thing later? Let's get going. Come on, start the engines, I'm already late!' Janey clapped her hands together.

'Look lady, I need this radio and it's not working. I think we might have a faulty antenna.'

'Do you mean *you* might have a faulty antenna,' she corrected. 'And why do you need the radio to drive the boat anyway?'

'I don't need it to drive the boat. I need it to send out a mayday call because we are out of fuel!'

Janey stood with her mouth open ready to say something but no words would come out.

Travis continued to fiddle with the wires and curse under his breath. 'Look, I'll try to explain it to you. After you retired for the night, I started up the engine and at first it fired up fine but then she suddenly died. Then I remembered asking Honey to go and ask Bill in the fuel shed for more cans for our trip, but then I got distracted by you and I somehow forgot to check that we actually had the fuel on board before we left the dock.'

'Distracted? By me?' Janey squealed.

'Yeah. Didn't you know the dress you're wearing is completely see-through when you stand with the sun behind you?'

Travis stuffed the wires back into the radio receiver and tapped it gently with the tip of his screwdriver. Suddenly it sprung into life. He could clearly hear someone speaking over the radio waves. It was the weather report. It might have taken him all night, but he had actually fixed it.

He gave out a little cheer to offer Janey a little hope, as she was still giving him a hard time.

*Is it broken? Can you fix it? Ya...da...ya...da!*

Boy, that woman was higher maintenance than his boat. He pitied the poor bastard who was marrying her. He'd noticed the rock she wore on her left hand; it had to be worth a pretty penny. Probably marrying a banker or a doctor or someone like that, he imagined. Although, to be fair, he did feel guilty about not having enough fuel on board for the journey. He didn't quite know how he'd come to miss that – it was certainly unprofessional of him and it was embarrassing. Then there was the radio malfunction; that was just plain spooky.

*Perhaps the woman was bad luck? That must be it. Some people just brought bad karma with them.*

Why he'd tried to impress her last night, he didn't really know? But he'd taken her to his favourite spot to watch the sun go down. It was his special place. He often stopped there to have his supper. It was off the radar, quite literally, and that's another reason he liked it. Anyway, the radio was all fixed now, he just has to reconnect the antenna and they were good to go. He could get Bill on the channel and get him to bring them out some fuel.

*Hah, and bang goes any profit on this trip!*

Then Janey suddenly leapt to her feet and grabbed the microphone off him.

'Hello – hello – hello – mayday – mayday – mayday,' she yelled, clicking the button on the side on the mike for all it was worth.

The only sound he heard after that was a small explosion.

Travis was incensed. He ran around the deck with his head in his hands for a couple of minutes before he shouted, 'You stupid, *stupid* bitch! Don't you realise what you've done? You've gone and fried it!'

'What? How *dare* you speak to me in that way.'

She clicked the button a few more times but the radio was totally dead. 'And how was I supposed to know that you hadn't fixed it properly when you shouted out "hurray" as if you had?'

He was so frustrated and angry that he actually wanted to throw her overboard.

*This woman was a sea-witch!*

'Look, I still had the antenna disconnected. You didn't give me a chance to reconnect it. I *had* fixed it. It *was* fixed. But then you caused a short circuit and blew it up!'

Then before she could ask him again *'if he could fix it',* he gave it to her straight. 'And this time, thanks to you, Lady Janey, it's unfixably fucked.'

A while later, despite her throbbing head and her desperate need for tea, Janey had a brain wave. She leapt into action, rummaging through her bag until she found her mobile phone. 'I've got it. I can save us. Look here, I have a phone. We can use it to send out a call. I just don't know why I didn't think of it earlier.'

A few minutes later, in frustration at not getting any signal, Janey tossed the phone overboard.

It was almost noon. Travis was drinking from a bottle of rum, and she was having to accept that she'd missed her chance to get Nola Nichols for the June cover and that Gwen would be furious and Mark would be worried about her.

The sun was intense as they sat on deck. There was very little shade. Below deck, it was oppressively hot and the confined space had made Janey feel even more nauseous, if that was at all possible. She took a couple more of Mark's pills to calm her rising hysteria. Travis handed her the bottle of rum to wash them down and, at that moment, it look all her strength of mind not to burst into tears.

'How long do you think it will it take them to find us?' she asked, handing him back the bottle.

Travis, seated on an upturned bucket, looked at her intently. 'Okay, the good news is that we have a perfectly good boat and a working engine. The bad news is that we have no fuel and a fried radio which means that we have no emergency transmitter with which to send out a distress signal.'

Janey blew her nose with her one remaining tissue. 'But I don't understand. Surely once the rescue services realise we are missing, they'll simply retrace our route from Antigua to Tortola and find us sitting here waiting to be rescued?'

Travis winced.

'What is it? Come on, what else? What haven't you told me?'

He shook his head. 'Well, you see, I took a little detour from our planned route because I wanted you to see all the BVIs at sunset, which means that we are not quite where we are supposed to be, so it could take some time for Air Sea Rescue to find us.'

'We are not where we are supposed to be because we are supposed to be on Tortola!' Janey yelled at him, even though her throat was burning from swigging neat rum.

He threw his arms into the air. 'There really is no pleasing you. I was just trying to throw in a perfect Caribbean sunset to make sure you got your five hundred fuckin' bucks worth!' he retaliated.

'Oh my gosh, we're going to die out here, aren't we? We are going to die of heatstroke.'

Travis suddenly got to his feet. 'No, we are *not* going to die! I'm the captain of this boat and I'll tell you what we are gonna do… We're gonna pull anchor and drift with the current on the high tide towards that island over there.' He pointed a finger over at Tit Island. 'And we are gonna gather up some supplies and despatch the lifeboat. And we are gonna sit on that beach under the shade of a palm tree and have something to eat and to drink until help arrives.'

He made it all sound like a jolly picnic rather than a marooned party.

Janey wasn't convinced. 'So, you mean that instead of dying of heatstroke here on the boat we are going to be castaways on a remote island and, just like Blackbeard's buccaneers, we will eventually die in an agony of thirst and starvation?'

At this, she couldn't hold it together any longer, and she burst into floods of tears.

Travis rolled his eyes heavenward. 'Oh, for Pete's sake, we aren't going to thirst or starve because I have plenty of supplies. Come with me and I'll show you.'

She followed him below deck. Instead of going in the direction of the cabin they went behind the ladder and into the hold.

'See?' he said, waving an arm with flourish across his bounty of cargo.

Janey was taken aback by the sight of boxes and bottles of rum, fresh fruit, tinned food, bottles of drinking water and even crates of cola. She turned to Travis in amazement. He was grinning at her proudly.

Indignant, she folded her arms in front of her chest. 'What I see here is a man who was clearly taking supplies over to Tortola *anyway*, and yet still charged me five hundred dollars in any case. What sort of boat captain are you anyway, sailing off across the sea without enough fuel with a fare paying passenger and with faulty radio equipment?'

Travis, embarrassed at having to face up to his failures, decided to ignore her and haul some of the supplies up on to the deck. Reluctantly, Janey felt she should offer him a hand, because whether he was a rubbish sea captain or not, he was the only means she had of surviving the hours, the days or the weeks, that they might be stuck together on Tit Island.


The lifeboat was an inflatable dinghy. Travis pulled a cord and it inflated itself. He set it onto the water and Janey climbed on board after first having changed into the only other clothes, aside from lingerie, that she had brought with her, which was a pair of shorts and a vest. He handed her a large heavy bag and several boxes all labelled 'Rum'.

'Are we gonna have a beach party?' she suggested sarcastically.

His eyes twinkled at her deviously. 'Arh, they might all be labelled rum,' he told her, 'but I've used these boxes to pack some supplies that we might need on the island… including rum.'

With boxes tightly packed around Janey, Travis checked over and secured *The Mermaid*, then he too climbed into the dinghy. He rowed while she held everything steady.

'What if the rescue plane flies over and sees *The Mermaid* but we are not on it?' Janey asked him nervously. 'Or what if it's after dark and we can hear them but they don't see us?'

'We can fire a flare. I have one here.' He indicated to the small orange gun held precariously in the waistband of his shorts. 'But I only have one shot, so it's to be used only if we have no other way of alerting them to our position.'

Janey nodded to show him she understood.

Travis had stripped to the waist for rowing. He took the oars and moved his lean body back and forward, flexing his powerful arms against the strength of the current that wanted to take them past the island and further out to sea. His quickly got into a rhythm that provided them with some speed.

After some twenty minutes or so, she could see they were heading directly towards a beach. It looked idyllic: white sand, palm trees, lapping waves upon the shore. It looked like the perfect romantic holiday retreat. Janey thought of Mark and wondered what he was doing right at that moment. *Did he even realise she was missing yet?*

# Chapter Five

Seventy-five nautical miles away on the island of Antigua, Mark was having his lunch. He was eating a chicken salad at the same time as reading a British newspaper. The paper was a day old but he perused it anyway. He was interrupted by the hotel's receptionist approaching his table in haste.

'Mr King. There is a telephone call for Miss Sinclair.' She held out a handset.

'Oh, okay. I'll take it.' He was surprised to hear Gwen's voice. 'Hey, Gwen, it's Mark.'

'Oh, Mark. I was hoping to speak to Janey but she's not answering her mobile phone. Is she there with you?'

Mark was taken aback. 'No, she left for Tortola yesterday to do your photo shoot.'

'Oh, well that's strange. It was all set for this morning but she didn't show up. Is everything okay over there?'

The tan Mark had been nurturing paled as he took in this information. 'She didn't show…?'

'No. The photo shoot was set for eight o'clock this morning. It was a small window of opportunity. Janey knew that Nola Nichols was booked on a flight out to London today.'

Mark checked his Rolex. 'It's after one pm here now, Gwen. I'll have to call you back.'

He disconnected the call and stood up, upturning his coffee cup, and he went straight to reception.

'I need to speak with the manager immediately. It's important,' he told the receptionist.

Leo, the hotel manager, appeared within seconds. 'What can I do for you, Mr King?'

Ten minutes later, Leo was off the phone to the harbour master on Tortola. He looked at Mark with grave concern. 'I'm afraid that *The Mermaid* is not there so we have alerted the coastguard to do an immediate search of the waters between here and Tortola.'

At this terrible news, Mark had to steady himself against the reception desk.

Leo immediately intervened to calm him. 'Please don't panic, Mr King. We will find them and I can assure you it will be soon.' He clicked his fingers and the receptionist jumped to attention. 'Quickly, fetch Mr King a glass of water.'

'Erm, if you don't mind,' Mark cut in sharply, 'I think I'd prefer a Scotch right now.'

He was then escorted to the bar by the concerned Leo, who continued to promise a speedy and successful conclusion to the mystery of the missing boat, its captain and passenger.

'I still have full confidence in Captain Mathews, and I'm sure we'll find that they have simply broken down in the water and are awaiting our assistance. Let me assure you, Mr King, we have the best search and rescue service in the world here in Antigua.'

Mark propped himself up on a bar stool, popped a couple of anxiety pills and drank the whisky straight down. Several hours later, he was still sitting there, waiting for news and drinking whisky, when he saw the Caribbean Goddess of Flowers from the night before approaching him from across the room, except that on this occasion she was wearing blue shorts and a white blouse.

'Senor King, I have been told that your girlfriend is missing with Travis Mathews on *The Mermaid?*' She spoke in a heavy and very sexy Latino accent.

Mark looked at her expectantly. 'Yes, that's right. Do you have news?'

'No, not yet. I fear we must wait a little longer. I'm Honey. I'm Travis's girlfriend. Perhaps we can keep each other company while the search is ongoing?'

'Yes, thank you. I must admit this is a very stressful time for me.'

'Yes,' she agreed, with a pained expression on her lovely face. 'It is for me too.'

'Well, despite the circumstances, it's nice to meet you, Honey. Although I do remember that we first became acquainted last night. Here, please, sit down.'

He pulled up a bar stool for her and blushed at recalling last night's show.

She smiled at him. 'Yes, I hope you didn't mind me dancing on your lap and binding your hands up in my flowers. It's a part of my routine.'

He shook his head and blushed even more. 'Can I get you a drink, Honey?'

She nodded. 'Si, gracias. I'll have a mojito.'

When Travis and Janey eventually reached the beach in the dinghy, they quickly clambered out and waded ashore. Together she and Travis carried the assortment of provisions onto the sand before dragging the small craft up the beach.

Curious, she asked Travis, 'What's in the big bag?'

'A tent for you, my lady, a hammock for me, and a few other things we might need.'

Janey had to admit that Travis seemed pretty well-organised and she had been more than grateful to him for pulling the confident captain speech, assuring her that they weren't going to die as castaways, just at the moment when she was about to fall apart.

A short time later, with the tent up and a fire going, Travis took a hessian sack, a snorkel and a mask and what looked to be a spear gun, from the big bag they had brought along.

'Going fishing?' she called after him as he made his way down the beach.

'Yeah. What's your favourite seafood, Janey?'

Janey pondered this for a moment. At the restaurant she and Mark went to every Friday night in Edinburgh, they had lobster on the menu. It was expensive and she had always longed to order it but never got the chance. 'Lobster!' she yelled to Travis.

He gave her the thumbs up and dived into the sea.

She watched him from the beach as he scouted around the rocks and under the water. Then he did a quick duck dive and disappeared. She happened to check her watch then applied her sun cream and waited.

After almost five minutes, she stood up in a panic.

There was no way that she could possibly have held her breath for as long. She struggled to do one minute underwater in her local swimming pool. Didn't people die if they were underwater for more than three minutes? She'd read that somewhere? It might have even been in her own magazine, when they'd featured pearl divers in the cold waters of Loch Fyne.

*Where was he? What if he had drowned? What if he had left her alone on this island?*

She gazed frantically out at the water. Then, just as she was about to have a full blown anxiety attack, he reappeared and came wading out of the surf with his mask on his head and a big grin on his face.

'No lobster I'm afraid, but just look at what I found.'

The fish he turned out of his canvas sack onto a flat rock was big and spiny and still moving.

'Don't you know how worried I was?' Janie yelled at him, waving her finger out to sea. 'Don't you think you could have at least warned me how long you'd be gone?'

'But… I was only gone for five minutes?'

'Yes, exactly. What are you, the man from Atlantis or something? Are you half fish? Do you have gills, or whatever it is that makes it possible for you to stay underwater for…' She checked her watch. '…five minutes and forty seconds?'

Travis's smile got even wider. 'Really? That's great. Hey, I just broke my own free-dive record.'

Janey stared at him in disbelief.

A moment later he was giving the fish he'd caught his full attention.

'I think that fish is still alive,' she observed, cringing as he took hold of his knife.

'Nah, it's just nerves twitching. I assure you it's dead, but don't touch it until I cut off the venomous spines.'

Janey stared at it in horror. 'Venomous?'

'Yeah, it's a lionfish and a big one too. Very tasty indeed. You are in for a treat.'

Janey took a step back as he began carefully removing the spines and then expertly gutting the fish. 'Lionfish are the scourge of the Caribbean,' he told her, 'and they are a real danger to the health of the reef. They will attack every fish they come across. They have no natural predators.'

She thought the fish looked disgusting. She couldn't imagine herself eating this creature. This looked nothing like the fish she was used to seeing, either on an iced slab in a supermarket or dressed on her plate in a restaurant.

'I'm sorry, Travis. You go ahead. I'm going to take a nap. I think I've had rather too much excitement for one day.'

He watched her walk slowly and despondently back to her tent. He knew she was feeling afraid and vulnerable. She was a tourist, after all, and he'd had to be brutally honest with her about their prospects of being found soon. They did have prospects, of course – this was the Caribbean Sea not the Pacific Ocean – but he expected it was going to take some time.

In fact, he'd heard stories of people being marooned on these islands for a very long time.

Amongst the Virgin Islands, you were never really out of sight of land, but with sixty islands in the chain and fifty-two uninhabited, that's what made it needle in a haystack territory. It was, of course, entirely his fault that they were in this mess. If he hadn't been trying so hard to impress her from the outset, he might have remembered the fuel and perhaps not even taken the scenic route.

He looked through a box and found his condiments: his jars of spices and food flavourings. He'd recently been to the 'spice island' of Grenada and stocked up. In his previous life in the States, he'd been a chef and owned a restaurant. Now that he was a boat captain instead, he still liked to cook, and he thought he might use this particular skill of his as a secret weapon to try to entice Janey back out of her tent.

The girl had to be hungry. She certainly looked hungry, in his opinion.


When early evening came around and Janey finally crawled out of her tent, a half-crescent moon had taken centre stage in a sky and there was a warm breeze blowing enticing smells of wood smoke and cooking in her direction. It made her realise that she hadn't eaten for a very long time and her stomach, sensing that food was near, was now growling voraciously.

Travis saw her approach. 'Dinner's almost ready.'

Inquisitive, she walked over to him. He was squeezing limes into a bowl and he had a row of little condiment bottles to his side. It seemed that Captain Travis was quite the cook for the smells coming from his pots were making her mouth water.

'Well, if there really is enough for two, then perhaps I should try the lion fish?'

Travis looked up and smiled. She noticed that he had a drop of sauce on his chin and she just managed to stop herself from being too familiar and reaching over to wipe it away for him.

'This marinade needs just one more dash of something spicy and then it will be perfect. Come on, sit down. There is plenty for two.'

Janey did as she was told. He laid out a towel between them, picnic style, and set out plates and cutlery. Then, shaking a large plastic container vigorously, he carefully poured out two mugs of the contents.

'Bottoms up,' he said, raising his mug to hers.

'Cheers,' said Janey, tipping what she was delighted to find was a strong and fruity rum punch down her parched throat. 'Oh, wow. That's really good!'

'Another?'

'Oh yes, please.'

After a few more rum punches and a plate full of sweet and sour flavoured lion fish, Janey was feeling far less stressed and even more impressed with Captain Travis Mathews. After all, they had plenty of food, they had lots of rum, they had fresh water and, well... they had each other.

She pondered on her thoughts. Travis was a bit rough round the edges but at least he had a confidence about him that made her feel safe. She wondered how Mark would have handled being castaway on an uninhabited island? Certainly not as calmly or as rationally as Travis had, but then again, Mark probably wouldn't have run out of fuel in the first place.

'So how long have you lived in the Caribbean?' she asked him.

He smiled at her smugly. 'Four years and I'm livin' the dream.'

'And you're American, right?'

He laughed and shook his head. 'No. Actually, I was born in the UK. My parents moved over to the States when I was a kid and that's where I grew up.'

'Where in the States?'

'Texas and then I lived in Florida for a while too. I was a chef and I owned a restaurant there.'

That accounted for the sexy southern accent and the cooking skills, she realised. 'And now, why the Caribbean?'

'Oh, I moved here for the same reasons most people do, to start my life over again. Now I transport goods between the islands, although usually more successfully than on this particular occasion, I might add.'

'And will you stay and maybe open another restaurant on Antigua?'

'If we ever get off this island you mean?'

Janey stiffened at his words but then saw he was looking at her with a glint of mischief and amusement in his eyes.

'I'm afraid that I don't share or appreciate your sense of pessimism, Captain.'

After a moment, in which he looked a little moody, he answered her question.

'Yeah, I'll stay. That's the plan for one day; a seafood restaurant perhaps, as I've got a boat. But it's complicated.'

A silence fell between them but she pleaded with him to go on. 'You can't just leave it like that. You have to tell me how complicated?'

'What, so that you can write all about it in your magazine, you mean?'

Janey shook her head. 'No way. In fact, you have my word that what is said on this island stays on this island.'

'Okay, I'll tell you. I was a partner in the restaurant with my best friend and my wife of ten years.'

Janey groaned. 'Oh, I'm so sorry. How did she die?'

Travis reeled at her conclusions. 'She didn't die and they were two different people. My wife was making out with my business partner who also happened to be my best friend!'

'Oh no! *That* kind of complicated? That's awful.'

'Yeah, it kinda was. I caught them together in the cold pantry. It was disgusting.'

Janey gasped at the awfulness. 'Do you have any kids?'

He shook his head. 'I always wanted them but I'm glad now that we didn't.'

'And so, what did you do after you caught them together?'

'What could I do? I sold out my part in the restaurant and I came here. I bought my boat and my house on the beach and now I have absolutely no complications.

'And what about friends? Are they allowed in your uncomplicated life?'

'Yeah, I have lots of friends. I'm a very friendly and sociable kinda guy.'

'Yeah, I kinda noticed.' Janey couldn't help herself but to mimic his slow drawl.

'Arh, then I assume you must be referring to the lovely Honey?'

Janey wondered if she really wanted to know the details of his relationship with the gorgeous girl on the boat, who had to be quite a few years younger than he was. She guessed Travis must be closer to forty than thirty, although it was entirely possible that his tanned skin and old sea-dog demeanour might have added on a few years.

He shrugged. 'We have a bit of fun, that's all.'

'Well, that's great,' she said all too quickly, before realising that a bit of fun might possibly the one thing that was lacking in her relationship with Mark. They always had a nice time together and they never ran out of stimulating conversation. But fun? No. Everything with Mark was too well planned and orchestrated to allow for much spontaneity. She made a mental note to herself that when she got out of this awful situation, she and Mark would somehow find a way to have lots of fun together in future. *If* she ever got out of this situation, that is.

Travis indicated towards her left hand and Mark's ring. 'I notice from that rock on your finger that you still have married life to look forward to, so I hope I haven't put you off too much?'

Janey stretched out her fingers and gazed at it. 'He proposed just yesterday. We've been together a few years, so I was sort of expecting it.'

'Then I wish you luck.'

She looked at Travis and smiled. 'Thank you.'

He reached over and took away her empty plate. 'Now, I have mango for dessert. It's a bit overripe, so it will be both messy and totally delicious.'

When they had finished eating the mango, they both had juice running down their chins. Janey looked around for a napkin but there wasn't one.

'Come on, it's time to wash up,' Travis told her.

She got to her feet, a little unsteadily, thinking that he meant the pots and plates, but he took her by the sticky hand and led her into the warm sea, where they waded in up to their knees and splashed about, washing their hands.

The sky was black and littered with the brightest stars that Janey had ever seen. She tipped her head back in wonder at the heavens. With the sea reflecting the starlight, it was almost impossible to see were the water finished and the sky began. It was like being in some kind of space observatory.

'Here, let me help you?' Travis said, pointing his finger to her face.

She laughed. 'Oh, do I still have some food around my mouth?'

He nodded and wiped one big salty wet finger gently over her upturned chin and then he showed her the small a piece of mango that had been stuck to it.

'Thank you, Travis.'

'You are very welcome,' he replied, his eyes locked into hers.

Janey found herself feeling unsteady again. She wobbled. He grabbed her hand, squeezing it.

'Don't worry, I gottcha,' he said softly, looking down at her.

'Thank you for the meal, Travis. It was very delicious and most appreciated.'

His lips curled into a slow smile and his eyes crinkled at the corners.

At that moment, she had a sudden urge to kiss him. Obviously, being castaway and drunk and grateful for his food was a dangerous mix. So she slipped her hand from his light grip.

'I wonder what time it is. I think it's probably really late.'

Travis looked up at the stars. 'No, it's just after midnight.'

'Really? You can tell that just by looking at the stars?'

'Sure. All the information you need is up there in the night sky. That's how the ancient mariners navigated their ships and reached their destinations on time without the aid of a computer.'

She stared at him and felt so glad that he actually knew such things.

'Can I interest you in a night cap?' he offered.

His offer was tempting, but she knew she'd be in trouble if she drank any more rum tonight.

'Thanks. But as it's after midnight, I'm more than ready to go sleep, so goodnight, Travis.'

She started to walk back up the beach, feeling his eyes on her every single step of the way.

'Thanks again!' she called out to him before she finally disappeared into her tent.

# Chapter Six

It was early morning, but the sun was beating down so hot that it was impossible for her to stay inside her tent any longer. Drenched in sweat, she crawled out on all fours and then looked around to find Travis. He was sleeping in the dinghy. His long arms and legs were hanging over the sides and an empty bottle of rum was balanced on his bare chest. He was snoring loudly.

She grabbed a bottle of drinking water and rummaged through her bag for some aspirin.

Travis grunted, waking himself up. 'Oh I feel like shit and we've got a lot to do today. We should get an early start.'

Janey handed him the water and the aspirin. 'Okay, I'm mystified. Tell me what exactly there is to do here that warrants an early start?'

He didn't answer straight away. He went down to the shore for a pee.

Janey looked the other way. She didn't need a pee and that must mean she was dehydrated.

When he came back, he pointed up to the two mountains high above them.

'These are the two highest points for miles around. If we were to fire the one flare that we have at our disposal down here on the beach, then I doubt it will be seen. My thoughts are that we should do it from high ground. Up there, there's far more chance of it being seen by other boats or by the search and rescue services.'

Janey looked up at the jungle-covered summits and considered his plan. It wouldn't be easy to get up there but his plan had merit. They certainly wouldn't want to blow their one and only chance at being seen from a distance by sending their flare fizzling off into the trees.

'Okay,' she agreed. 'Let's get some water bottles and some food together. It could take us a while to reach the top.'


The coastguard and the Air Sea Rescue continued their search at first light. Yesterday afternoon's investigations along the route between Antigua and Tortola had not been successful. *The Mermaid*, Miss Sinclair and Captain Mathews were still nowhere to be seen.

Leo, the hotel manager, knocked on Mark's room door at six am.

'Mr King, there is a helicopter going up in twenty minutes. They say that if you'd like to, you can join the search today.'

Mark rolled groggily from the bed and opened the door of his villa.

'Yes, thank you, Leo. I'll get dressed.'

He staggered about, trying to drag on his tailored shorts while his stomach rolled with nausea from last night's whisky and now from this morning's fear of flying in a helicopter. But with Janey still missing, he was determined to overcome his own shortcomings and his self-inflicted hangover, in order to be there when she was found.

Janey was such a fragile woman who didn't do well outside her own secure environment, and so he didn't expect she'd be handling all of this very well at all. However, when it was over, it might teach her an important lesson for when they were married. She would do well in future to heed his advice, rather than to ignore him and go off on some silly wild goose chase, on the orders of someone other than her husband.

Fifteen minutes later, he was climbing inside what looked to be a small fish bowl with rotor blades on the top. Inside, it was cramped and hot and noisy. He took the bench seat behind the two pilots and strapped himself in. They handed him a headset with a microphone, so he would be able to hear their communications. He was distracted from throwing-up his last two remaining anxiety pills by Honey running towards the helicopter.

'Hi, everyone,' she said, climbing inside the small space in an impossibly short skirt and low cut top. She sat next to Mark on the narrow seat and pressed her bare leg against his.

The pilots smiled lustily at her and both fought over helping her with her seat belt.

'Oh dear, I'm afraid you don't look so good this morning, Mark,' she told him.

'Oh, I'll be okay. I'm just sick with worry about Janey, that's all,' he explained.

They flew over water for hours, looking down until their eyes were swimming in their heads.

One of the problems they had in searching for *The Mermaid*, was identifying one specific boat out of so many, when the Caribbean was one of the top sailing and boating destinations in the world. From the air, with the exception of the tall sailing boats, they all looked pretty much the same. Any one of them could have been *The Mermaid*.

One of the pilots spoke into the radio. 'Mermaid, Mermaid, this is Air Search and Rescue. What is your position? Over.' He repeated this two more times but there was no response.

'We must assume their radio is out but that they may still be able to hear us,' the pilot explained.

'Yes, please keep trying,' Mark begged.

'We will, Mr King. If they know we're looking for them they will have their flare ready.'

'Their flare?' Mark queried.

'Yes, they will have a flare gun. With so many boats on the sea and anchored up in small coves and harbours, it's likely they will spot us and not the other way round. So look out for their signal.'

Mark and Honey turned to each other and smiled. It seemed that there was hope after all.

Beyond the curve of the white sand beach, it looked to be all dense jungle. The undergrowth was so tall that it was almost impossible for them to see exactly where they were heading. Travis led the way. Janey kept her eyes trained on the ground and where she was putting her feet, so that she didn't stumble. She wore canvas shoes but they were no protection against the rough grasses, the sharp slippery rocks, and the occasional mud filled and smelly swamp.

It was stiflingly hot and humid. Their bodies and clothes were soaked with sweat. Their hair was wet and matted to their heads. After a while, Janey's patience wore thin and she got fed up with everything that Travis was pushing back only to slap her in the face.

'Come on, these are the days of equality. Why don't I lead and you follow me for a change?'

Travis stopped and turned. He wiped his hot wet brow with his dirty forearm and handed over his compass and the machete blade he had been using to chop through the undergrowth that had otherwise refused to yield.

'Watch you don't hurt yourself,' he warned, indicating towards the blade. 'We don't want you chopping off your own arms and legs, do we?'

Janey could hardly lift the blade, never mind swing it. He had made it look unreasonably easy. But she steeled herself and struggled on while Travis trudged in her footsteps. She made sure she swung a few large items of vegetation his way too but, to his credit, he didn't complain.

Soon they entered a clearing. Janey picked up the pace a little and when she came across an idyllic blue lagoon and a waterfall, she squealed with delight.

'Oh wow! Look what I found.'

'Look what *you* found?' Travis groaned. He started to remove his shirt and his shoes.

Janey leapt into the lagoon with hers still on. 'Oh, this is fabulous,' she told him from the clear cool water.

'Watch out for sea snakes!' Travis yelled, just before he dived in smoothly and came up to the surface right next to her.

'Oh my goodness, really?' She had wanted to swim down into the cool water again but now she wasn't so sure. Who knows what creatures were down there. She looked about her nervously and then felt something wrapping itself around her leg. 'Oh my… I think you're right. I think there *is* a snake in here!'

Travis laughed. 'No. I was just kidding around. This is a freshwater lagoon so no sea snakes. He reached down and pulled up a handful of pondweed. See?'

Janey groaned with relief

'Look, Janey, I know we're not on Tortola where we should be right now but we're not in any immediate danger here, so how about for the next couple of hours or so we just forget we are marooned and let's enjoy it instead? I mean, you are on vacation, after all.'

She laughed at the idea. The coolness of the water and the closeness of his body at that moment was making her head spin.

'What? You mean we pretend to be at a spa retreat or something?'

'Yeah, why not. Let's just chill out here and wait to be rescued. Hell, I bet they even find us before nightfall.'

Janey shrugged. Maybe he was right. Getting upset and stressed out certainly wasn't going to help.

Travis headed over to the waterfall for a hydro-massage while Janey lay on her back in the water with her arms and legs splayed out. She thought back to the feature she'd put together for last month's issue of *Hot Scot*. It was on luxury spas and remembered how much she'd wished she could be so lucky to retreat to one. Yet here she was, surrounded by the therapeutic sound of flowing water and appreciating the feeling of warmth from the sun as it sent sparkling sunbeams through the diffused light of the tree canopy. She inhaled deeply the aromatic fragrance of the tropical jungle and opened her eyes to stare up into the mists above the tumbling waterfall and at all the colours of the rainbow in the bluest of skies.

She floated in the lagoon feeling weightless and free. This really was paradise.

But after about an hour of this encumbered bliss, Janey began to worry again. Was it fair for her to be enjoying herself so much when Mark was worried sick about her right now? When right this minute, so many people would no doubt be involved in a frantic and expensive search and rescue operation?

No. They really should be doing their part and everything possible to be found. They should be trying to get to the top of the mountain to set off their flare.


It seemed that the only way to progress any further on their uphill trek was to find a way of climbing up the side of the waterfall, as any alternative route looked far too steep, and featured impossible to tackle overhanging crags and dense vegetation that hung down like hangman's ropes.

'Come on, we can do this. Let me show you how,' Travis said, and demonstrated.

Janey watched him placing his feet and fingers into gaps in the rock face and haul himself up like he was on a climbing wall. Janey wasn't so sure she could do it, mainly because she was terrified of heights, especially precarious ones where a single foot wrong could prove instantly fatal.

'Come on, Janey. It's easy.'

While she stood hesitating below, she could see Travis was already halfway up.

'Easy for you maybe!' she hissed.

Fearing being left alone by him far more than fearing the climb, and with her whole body shaking violently, she followed him up the side of the waterfall. She clung to the rocks with her fingers, some stones jutted out and were uncomfortably sharp and some were slippery smooth. She pushed herself upward on quivering legs, taking great mouthfuls of air, and at other times realising she was holding onto her breath for far too long. Her fingernails snapped off one by one and her knees were grazed and stung.

When she reached the top, and Travis's strong arms hauled her over the final rock and onto the safety of the ledge, Janey had never felt so euphoric. She had never achieved anything like this before. It felt fantastic to face her fears. She did a little dance, wiggling her bottom and waving her arms while whooping loudly.

Travis laughed and clapped his hands. 'Yes, you did, little lady, you most certainly did.'

And then he did the most unexpected thing, he pulled her into his arms and he kissed her hard on her mouth. It was the most urgent kiss she'd ever experienced in her life. She was so shocked that, for what seemed an age, she didn't actually do anything to stop him, and instead, she wantonly allowed his hot, salty and so moist mouth to grind down on hers.

When she gathered her wits about her and opened her mouth to object, he pushed his tongue inside. Not in a creepy way, like when Mark forced his hard tongue deeply into her mouth and made her gag, but in a very sensuous way that turned her lower belly into liquid fire.

Eventually, at some point, breathless as their lips parted, she found the strength to push him away and take in a huge gulp of air.

Then she stared at him in disbelief.

He was smiling down at her, albeit a little bashfully. 'Do I need to apologise?' he asked, licking his lips as if savouring the taste of her.

She wiped her lips with the back of her hand and shook her head. 'No, but please don't ever do it again.'

They continued walking uphill; Travis resuming the lead. They didn't speak. The climb was so steep that it took every bit of energy in their bodies and every ounce of breath from their lungs, but if this was the only way of being saved from this island, Janey knew she had to find the strength from somewhere to reach the top of the mountain and to get back down to the beach again before dark.

At the summit, the pointed nipple peak, they stood in triumph, trying to get their breath back.

This time, Travis did the little dance, mimicking Janey's by wiggling his bottom and waving his arms.

She laughed and cheered him on but she didn't kiss him, even though the memory of his kiss was still burning in both her brain and her lower belly.

They sat next to each other on a tussock and took in the vista. They could easily see *The Mermaid* moored just off the headland of the cove where they were camped. They could see every island in the chain that was the British Virgin Islands and beyond to the US Virgin Islands too. Travis took out his binoculars and scanned the sea, a full 360 degrees.

In the far distance, there were tiny boats and miniature sails, but everything and everybody was so far away from them that the chance of someone seeing their flare as it lit up the sky for just a few moments would be practically nil.

'I just don't believe it!' Travis yelled angrily. 'I was so sure. I was so convinced there'd be a rescue plane going over, or a boat or a cruise ship going by close enough to see our signal and to respond. I'm sorry, Janey. I dragged you all the way up here for nothing, because we can't risk sending off our only flare today.'

Janey looked at him and felt uneasy. He was usually so cool and composed. She didn't like him like this at all. He was aggravated and upset. She wanted her confident captain back again.

'No, it wasn't for nothing,' she said softly. 'I mean, look at the view, it's simply stunning. It has absolutely been worth the climb. Why don't we sit for a while and have our picnic here?'

So, for a while they sat quietly, munching their food and sipping water until rested and replenished. Then Travis stood up and suggested that they start the journey back.

'We certainly don't want to be stuck in the jungle after dark.'

Janey got to her feet and turned for one last look at the incredible view, with the intention of imprinting it in her memory forever; something good to remember about the island when they were rescued and taken back to the real world. Only, what she saw next caused her to shriek out in excitement.

'Omigosh! Look, Travis, there's a boat!' She did her happy dance again

Travis immediately got his binoculars out and focussed on the big boat that was anchored just off the reef and the outboard that was pulling up alongside *The Mermaid*. He stood very still, watching carefully and then he swore loudly.

'Oh fuck! Fucking hell!'

Janey stopped her dancing, jolted by his language.

*Where had that outburst just come from?*

'What is it? You are scaring me. Tell me, what's going on?' she pleaded.

'Pirates. Robbers. Thieves. Call them what you will, they are looting my boat!'

Janey's eyes almost popped out of her head as she strained them in the direction of the two boats.

*Pirates…?*

'You mean as in arrrgggghhh…?'


They got back down the mountain and to the beach in record time but the pirate boat was gone. Travis wasted no time in dragging the inflatable dinghy into the water and rowing towards his boat. He cussed and cursed as he rowed, thinking now that he was a fool to have gone ashore.

He'd known there were pirates in these waters but had assumed that floating *The Mermaid* over the razor-sharp reef surrounding the headland at high tide would have provided her with an element of protection while they were ashore. This tactic had worked to a point, as the thieving bastards hadn't actually been able to get close enough with their main boat to tow her away, but they'd reached her using a RIB – a rigid inflatable boat - and were sure to have tried to start her up, realising she was out of fuel. Hell, he'd even left the key in the ignition. He'd been too lax. It was a case of thinking it couldn't happen to him but, of course, it could. This wasn't the first time he'd lost everything, but he was damned if he was going to let these pirate thieves come back on the high tide and take his boat.

Once he reached *The Mermaid*, he climbed on board and to his dismay, saw that anything of any value had been stripped away and stolen. In the hold, all his cargo had gone, and in his cabin his personal items were missing too. His box, the one in which he'd kept the few material things that actually meant something to him, had been taken by the looters. *The watch his father had given him on his twenty-first birthday, the photo of his parents' on their wedding day, his mother's ring and his own wedding ring – all gone.* Fury was enough to describe his anger.

Feeling sick because his day simply couldn't get any worse, he went back up on deck and stood there for a moment. The only sound he could hear was that of water slapping against the hull.

He looked out to sea and saw nothing but the dark line of the horizon, broken only with the shadows of distant islets. On the beach he could see Janey, sitting at the water's edge, looking like a mermaid, watching and waiting for his return.

His heart felt as heavy as an anchor with the weight of his responsibility.

An hour later he was back on the island. The sun had gone down and it was dark. So was his mood. He threw an empty cool box from the boat onto the beach.

Janey looked at him in wild-eyed panic. 'What happened?'

'They took everything, and I mean everything,' he told her. 'They stripped her down.'

'What are we going to do now, Travis? What will we eat? How will we survive?'

There was no sense now in protecting her from the awful truth, as without his boat full of supplies, they were probably going to die on this island in an agony of thirst and starvation.

Turning on her in bitter frustration, he felt his patience snap, and he pointed his finger at her accusingly.

'Just why the hell do you expect me to have all the answers, lady? Why don't you go and see if you can find some of your own answers for a change and get off my fucking back.' Immediately he'd said it, he wanted to take it back but it was too late.

Janey, no doubt feeling more afraid than she'd ever felt before, had burst into tears and run into her tent, from where he could hear the sound of her sobbing late into the night.

# Chapter Seven

The helicopter returned just as the sun was going down. Mark and Honey climbed out of it feeling despondent and exhausted. 'I just can't understand how we haven't found them by now. I mean, where can they be?' Mark wailed.

Honey linked her arm through his and suggested they both needed a drink.

Back at the hotel, they sat discussing the tensions of the day, the fruitless search, and the new area that they would be searching over the following day.

'Only, to me, it seems so unlikely they would have travelled so far west,' Mark told Honey.

'I think we have to trust that the rescue services know what they are doing,' she said, shrugging her delicate shoulders and continuing to sip her cocktail through a straw.

Mark watched how sexily she pursed her lips.

After several more drinks, they both agreed that they were too tired and upset to eat, and decided to call it a night. Mark walked Honey back to her room at the back of the hotel in the staff quarters where she was currently staying. 'You want to come inside?' she asked him.

'No. Thank you. I won't. I just wanted to be sure you were okay.'

'I'm missing Travis and I hate to be alone. If you stay here tonight and we can keep each other company. We both need emotional support at this time.'

Mark stared at her with his eyes wide. 'Me? Stay here? With you?'

His eyes slid across the room in the direction of the bed. There was only one bed and the room was small and sparsely furnished, with no room for a sofa. He couldn't possibly stay here with Honey tonight.

'Yes, with me,' she answered softly, removing her bra in front of him.

Mark shook his head. He dragged his gaze up from her big, beautiful, firm breasts to her large pleading and teary eyes, and he took in a deep breath. 'No. I'm sorry, Honey. I really can't'


The following morning, Janey would have much preferred to have stayed in her tent in order to have avoided facing Travis, but the sun was already shining down so intently that she had no choice but to climb out of it red-eyed and groggy and with her head pounding.

During the heat of the night, she had been going over and over in her mind all the events of the previous few days: the holiday, her engagement, the impromptu photo shoot, Travis kissing her so passionately and so unexpectedly, and his harsh words to her last night. And, when she'd eventually stopped crying, she'd come to a life affirming conclusion.

She had decided that Travis was right. It was about time that she found her own answers, her own solutions, and took some real responsibility for herself. She wasn't a girl any more. She was a grown woman and she had to stop relying on a man to make her feel safe and secure. No matter whose fault it was, she and Travis were in this situation together and they had to find away to pull together and survive. She didn't want to be a burden to him. She didn't want to be a wimp or a hanger-on. She needed to find the woman she had been in the jungle yesterday and ditch the pathetic whining bitch she'd been on the beach last night.

Travis saw her coming out from the tent and he stood up. He had a mask and snorkel on his head and a look of concern on his face.

'Janey, I want you to know, I'm really sorry about last night.'

She glanced at him through teary swollen eyes and noticed him wince.

'I had no right to speak to you that way,' he continued. 'It's just that I really hate it when you act all feeble and delicate because… well, when you climbed up that waterfall yesterday despite being terrified, you showed me that you are a lady who knows how to look after herself.'

His honestly was brutal. She sat down in the sand and wondered if there was any water to quench her thirst.

Then he shrugged and pointed his spear. On the end of it was a lobster. 'Anyway, look… I went and caught your breakfast.'

This had to be the most sincere apology she'd ever had. Not that she'd ever had that many, as all the men that she'd known hadn't ever been big on being sorry. She nodded, and he let out the breath he'd been holding onto.

'Phew, well, that's a relief. I'm gonna cook this beauty up for you right now over the fire, so if you want to go and wash up, I'll have it all ready for when you get back.'

Janey wandered off in the direction of the sea. She needed to pee and she needed to cool off.

She watched Travis from the water. He had the lobster meat quickly threaded onto skewers over the fire and he was basting it with one of the sauces from his kitchen tin. A strange feeling of warmth flooded through her. He had apologised to her and now he was cooking her breakfast. Not only that, he had gone out and caught her favourite food before she'd even woken this morning.

Travis Mathews, she decided, was a remarkable man. He spoke bluntly but he had been right to do so, because she'd behaved quite pathetically, and he'd been really upset because his boat had been ransacked. She decided that it was really her who needed to apologise to him, but that she would do it with actions, rather than mere words.

They ate their lobster breakfast and then took stock of their remaining supplies. They were low on drinking water but Janey reminded him of the freshwater supply they'd discovered the previous day. 'We could take turns in fetching water from the lagoon,' she suggested.

Travis eyed her curiously. 'Assuming we aren't rescued today. We have to stay optimistic.'

'Oh, I'm optimistic.' She smiled. 'I'm just thinking up a few contingency plans.'

As she helped him pack their few remaining provisions into the cool box, Travis seemed distant for a few moments. She guessed from the furrows ingrained in his brow that he was thinking about his boat and the pirates.

Then he looked at her and said, 'You do know that they'll be coming back on the high tide tonight, don't you, Janey?'

His tone, a warning rather than a statement, sent an icy shiver down her sweat-soaked back.

'You think? Why? What for? Do you mean, coming back for us?' Suddenly she was all aquiver again at the thought of being kidnapped or killed by pirates. These weren't handsome sea-dogs or colourful pirates either, like Johnny Depp in the *Pirates of the Caribbean* movie; these were hard-nosed, gun-toting, stop at nothing, modern-day thieves and murderers.

Travis shook his head. 'No, they'll be coming back for the boat but they won't risk running into the reef to tow her away, so they're likely to be back at sundown with fuel. We must be ready to intercept them.'

Janey fought hard to find the woman she had been in the jungle yesterday.

'But there are more of them than there is of us,' she pointed out.

Travis narrowed his eyes. 'Yeah, so we are gonna have to think up something clever.'

There was a moment or two of silence between them as they both tried to think cleverly.

'I think I've got an idea how we might do it,' she suddenly blurted out. 'We need to create a distraction to get them off *The Mermaid* once they've fuelled her up, so we can get on board and take her back.'

Travis wrapped one burly arm around her shoulders and gave her a side hug, almost lifting her off her feet. 'Hey, that's my girl!'


Mark was woken by a banging noise on the door. Before he opened his eyes, he guessed it would be Leo, waking him up so that he could join the search again today. He sat up in the bed and stretched himself. 'Okay, okay, I'm coming!'

It was only then that he remembered he wasn't in his own beach-front suite, but in a small staff bedroom at the back of the hotel. It was Honey's room and she was waking up beside him. Naked.

She yawned and then yelled out as the banging on the door came again. 'Okay, we are coming.'

Mark felt immediately sick. He watched as Honey left the bed, wrapping a sarong around herself as she went to the door to speak to Leo.

Mark dived under the sheet to hide.

Once Leo had gone, Honey told him to hurry. 'They are widening the search today. We must be ready in fifteen minutes.'

Mark groaned, remembering the night before when he had said no to Honey's advances only to knock on her door a few moments later, to take her to bed and have what had to be the most energetic sex he'd ever had in his life. *But how could he have done all of that when he was engaged to be married to Janey?*

Then he wondered if Janey was still alive, and how he would ever be able to look her in the eye again knowing what he'd done.

'I might not go today. I don't feel too good. I can go tomorrow and that would give you a break too,' he called to Honey.

Honey dashed out from the bathroom to wriggle into a pair of tiny shorts and vest style top.

She shrugged. 'That might not be possible *Chico*, because after today, if they still find nothing, they will call off the search. You know that, right?'

Mark look at her in dismay. 'Oh. No, I didn't know that.'

Janey and Travis had stacked up all the boxes they'd had their water and provisions in to make them look tall and visible on the beach. They put all the rum labels to the front and filled the few rum bottles they'd consumed with a brown muddy-looking concoction and placed them where they could be seen, in order to fool the pirates into thinking all the boxes were full.

'If they think we have more rum here, they'll come ashore to get it,' Janey explained.

'And then we'll sneak onto *The Mermaid* from behind the headland and take her back,' Travis enthused. 'We just have to be sure they don't see our rum decoy until after they've fuelled her up.'

'How fast can *The Mermaid* go?' Janey asked, while considering their get-away.

Travis frowned. 'Not quite fast enough to outrun their big old rusty sea-bucket unfortunately, so we'll have to think of a way of stalling them, but leave that to me.'

The plan he eventually concocted was to carry the dinghy over the hill to the headland in daylight, so they could launch it from the beach on the other side at sundown. That way, Travis explained to her, they could reach *The Mermaid* and wouldn't be seen by the pirates until it was far too late and they'd made their get away.

'Why can't we simply sail the dinghy around the headland?' Janey queried, thinking it would be a lot quicker and much easier for them than carrying a dinghy through the jungle.

'Simply because we can't risk going over that coral reef at low tide; it would slice up the inflatable and we'd sink only to be sliced up ourselves in the swell.'

Janey appreciated his point and then tried to understand the rhythm of the tides. It was complicated. Travis had explained that some tides were higher or lower than others, depending on the phases of the moon, and that's how he knew exactly when the pirates would return.

Travis laughed. 'Hah! To think that those pirates are bringing us the one thing we need to get off this island. It's a sweet irony, don'tcha think?'

Janey growled in hearty agreement. 'Aye, we'll teach them pesky pirate sea-dogs a lesson or two.'

While they were planning to be away from the beach taking the dinghy over to the headland, they kept their decoy boxes well hidden, using Janey's tent as a tarpaulin and covering it with palm leaves. They had deflated the dinghy but, despite it being rolled and compacted into a more manageable size, realistically it was still far too heavy for them to carry the considerable distance over the hill. It seemed that Stage One of their plan had a fatal flaw.

'Okay. We need to make a raft and drag it over the hill,' Travis decided.

So he cut some bamboo poles with his machete and she cut the palm leaves. It was a team effort and Janey worked tirelessly while keeping an eye on Travis, whom she could hardly keep her eyes off because he was handsomely stripped to the waist. Then they tied the deflated boat onto it with the rope they had brought ashore with them.

Travis also carried a backpack with the compressor in it, so they could easily inflate the boat once they were in position, and Janey made a kind of utility belt for herself out of tree vines, so that she could carry several bottles of drinking water but still keep her arms and hands free.

They both knew this plan was going to be arduous and not without risk, but it was likely to be their only way off getting off this island. Besides, they couldn't just sit back and let *The Mermaid* be taken. So they set off. It was much later in the morning than they had anticipated when they put their arms through the harnesses they'd made to enable them to drag the boat along, but they pulled and strained until they got it to move.

Pulling it across the sand was incredibly hard work. It was like wading through treacle and trying to move an unmovable object. Once they got to the edge of the jungle, they followed the path up the mountain they'd cleared the day before. Janey was glad of the tree canopy overhead that offered them some shade from the intensity of the sun during what was now the hottest part of the day.

They hardly spoke as they pulled the raft in tandem. When they got stuck, and their load seemed to get snagged on branches and rocks every few minutes, they stopped and cleared it. Then Travis counted, 'One, two three, heave…' so that they both pulled together as effectively as possible.

Making slow progress through the jungle, Janey tried to ignore the pain in her shoulders, the pounding headache she had developed from straining her neck muscles, and the sweat rolling out from every pore in her body. She racked her brain as to how they would tackle climbing the waterfall with the boat once they reached it. She hoped Travis would have a clever plan for that.

Once they reached the waterfall, Travis pointed out the hanging vines Janey had previously thought looked like hangman's ropes.

'I'm gonna climb up there and cut down those vines,' he told her, 'so that we can use them to haul the boat up the side of the waterfall.'

Janey watched in admiration as Travis climbed and swung nimbly on his strong arms up the rock face to reach the vines from the overhang. Once he had cut them all down, Janey gathered them up from where they had dropped to the ground and wound them around her shoulders. Travis climbed down again and they both set to work, knotting and attaching them to their makeshift raft.

Janey watched as he demonstrated all the clever and secure seafaring knots that he knew. She learned quickly from him and he encouraged her to tie some for herself. To her secret shame and embarrassment, she really enjoyed him sitting closely behind her with his legs stretched out either side of hers, as he instructed her on the hitch knot.

'Well, if anyone back in Edinburgh ever asks me if I know how to tie a midshipman's hitch, now I can say that yes, I do,' she said proudly, holding up her knotted rope.

With the vine lines attached to Travis's waist, they climbed up the side of the waterfall. He took the lead and Janey followed him carefully, but nowhere near as tentatively as she had the last time.

This time, she had her wits about her and she was in a state of high alert, because she knew that once they were at the top, they would need to act as a team in hauling up the heavy boat on its bamboo raft. This was no time for a crisis of confidence or the place for girlish nerves.

They also needed to work together keep the raft level, so that it didn't tip. At the same time they had to watch out for sharp rocks, which might tear the sides of the boat, rendering it useless.

Finally, after what felt like an age of straining and pulling and limb ripping agony, they managed to get the boat to the plateau at the top. Once they had secured it, they both collapsed onto the ground, groaning and panting with exhaustion.

'We bloody well did it!' Travis exclaimed with a great hoot of satisfaction. 'And you have amazed me once again, Janey Sinclair. I had no idea you were that damned strong or that bloody determined.'

Janey laughed a dry rasp from her parched throat. 'Believe me, neither did I!'

After they'd got their breath back, drank some water and refilled their water bottles from the falls, they started to move across the headland and towards the small cove on the other side of the hill. It was easier going on the flat headland and cooler now thanks to the cloud cover rolling in from the east. They collected some food as they went along. Travis pointed out a breadfruit, a couple of bananas, a coconut and an avocado.

Janey also noticed he was keeping a keen eye on the weather.

'I think we might be in for a storm,' he told her, 'so we'd be wise to find somewhere to shelter tonight in case we can't get back to the beach.'

'Will a storm stop the pirates coming back?' she asked him, worried at the possibility of things not coming together exactly as they'd planned.

He nodded. 'Yeah. It's likely they'll wait until tomorrow if the sea's too rough tonight.'

They'd reached the cove on the other side of the hill. It had taken them far longer than they'd thought and it was now much later in the day than they'd planned. Janey looked around for somewhere they might shelter.

'Look. Over there. Is that a cave?' She pointed to the top of the beach where the cliffside vegetation almost hid a gaping hole in the rock face.

They began dragging their raft and supplies towards it. Travis crawled inside with his torch to check for snakes, spiders and scorpions. Only once he'd shouted 'All clear' did Janey enter.

She thought it smelt funny. It was damp and musty and cold and dark in there.

'Phew, did something die recently?' she asked.

*Like maybe the last people to be castaway on this island?*

'It's a bat cave,' Travis explained. 'What you can smell is guano. That's bat shit, to you and me.'

She held her nose and thought she'd rather be outside in the rain than inside getting covered in bat shit. 'I think we should take turns to be on lookout tonight, just in case those pirates do turn up.'

Travis looked at her in amusement. 'Aye aye, first mate.'

Janey turned to him curiously. 'Really, I'm your first mate?'

'Yeah, I reckon you earned it. Consider yourself promoted from pain-in-the-arse tourist to senior deckhand.

She beamed at him. 'Aye aye, captain. As first mate, I'll take the first watch.'

# Chapter Eight

It was late afternoon when Mark officially heard they were calling off the search. He'd then had to speak on the phone to his own family, to Janey's mother and father, and to Gwen, Janey's boss, whom he practically had to talk off the ledge of the *Hot Scot Magazine* building because she felt so guilty for sending Janey off on her deadly assignment.

Feelings of guilt haunted him too. He felt like a terrible fraud mourning Janey's death, when he'd been unfaithful to her while the search was still ongoing, and when there had still been a glimmer of hope of her being found alive. Was this terrible tragedy in his life something he unwittingly deserved?

In contrast, Honey did not seem to understand his angst or to believe in any kind of karma, and so had taken his refusal to spend another night in her bed as a personal insult.

He was now trying to get drunk, except that it wasn't working. No matter how much whisky he drank, it seemed that his guilty heart could not be numbed.

Leo came and sat with him for a while. The two men didn't speak much but Mark was grateful for his company. Leo did explain that there would be memorial service on the beach in memory of Janey and Travis and that he should, as Janey's fiancé, think about saying a few words.

'I will, of course, also speak to Honey, and suggest she does the same in memory of Travis.'

Mark thanked him and signalled the bar tender for another drink.

Inside the cave, Travis had made a fire. He had also prepared their meal, while Janey took first watch for returning pirates. Outside, it was getting dark and the sky was getting angrier. Black clouds were rolling in fast and rumbled with thunder and occasionally flashed with lightning.

In the distance, towards the east, Janey watched as another storm system developed and forked lightning bolts lit up the line of the horizon. She'd never seen a tropical storm before and if these two weather fronts met tonight, as Travis had warned, then they were going to be in for the mother of all storms. She was both fascinated and terrified all at the same time.

Travis came outside to join her.

'We'll eat out here before the rain comes,' he told her, handing her a large 'leaf' plate and a selection of vegetables. He'd cooked the breadfruit like a baked potato in the fire's embers and used banana skins as tinfoil.

'Just how do you know how to cook like this?' she asked, while dipping into the soft tasty breadfruit and eating it with her fingers. 'This is absolutely delicious.'

'My granny. She was an amazing cook. With just a couple of potatoes and a few scraps, she could do wonders.'

'Well, she taught you well. Please thank her for me.'

Travis looked solemnly into what remained of his own breadfruit.

Janey rolled her eyes at her tactlessness. 'Oh, I'm sorry. She's dead, isn't she?'

He nodded. 'Yes, but she was *very* old when she died.'

Janey looked relived. 'Ah, so she'd had a good life?'

'Hell, no. She had a very hard life. My dad was the youngest of her twelve kids.'

But as Janey was about to ask more about his father and indeed his mother, if only to get out of the hole she was digging for herself, it began to rain. Not just a few drops of fair warning either, but a sudden downpour of almost biblical proportions that had them leaping up to take shelter inside the smelly old cave. As they peered out and watched, the wind whipped up. The storm raged and thunder claps rumbled overhead while corresponding lightning bolts struck down angrily at the sea.

'The storm's right overhead,' Travis told her.

'Oh wow! Did you see that?' Janey jumped back as a streak of lightning struck the water.

At this, they went further back into the cave to sit next to the fire and feed it with wood and sticks, while orange light and dark shadows leapt and danced on the walls behind them.

After a while, once Janey had become more accustomed to the acrid smell, it became quite a cosy place to rest. They'd agreed that there was no way that the pirates would be back tonight, as even cut-throat thieves wouldn't risk being electrocuted at sea. So they settled down to relax for a few hours and get some rest.

'You know, I wish we had some rum,' Travis said wistfully.

'I wish I had a bottle of wine,' Janey said, sighing and closing her eyes, imagining the fruity notes of a chilled Chardonnay on her tongue and the feeling of it sliding down her throat.

Mark had always ordered red wine at room temperature because that's what he liked, whereas she much preferred to drink a chilled white. She decided that when she got back, *if* she ever got back, she would be more assertive and tell him that it was okay for them to be different.

'Come here…' Travis offered. He was sitting with his long legs stretched out in front of him and with his back propped against the raft. He had one arm lifted up and he was indicating to her that she should lie next to him. 'Come on. I promise not to kiss you again. You are quite safe with me.'

She regarded him cautiously at first but then decided it would be rather nice to snuggle in and feel warm and safe. So she sat down next to him and welcomed the security of his big arm around her. She listened to his heart beating steadily in his chest and couldn't help but think again about the time he had kissed her. Something she'd thought about a lot since it had happened.

'Thank you. I do feel safe with you, Travis, and I have to be honest and tell you that I really liked you kissing me.'

He gave her an affectionate squeeze. 'I really liked kissing you too.'

She felt his chest rise under her resting head before he asked the next and obvious question.

'So why, if we both liked it, don't we kiss some more. It's only natural?'

She sighed and wondered how it was possible to feel what she felt for Mark, her fiancé, and yet still have this raw and passionate longing to make love with another man? Then she looked down at her engagement ring. 'Because it's best we don't start what we naturally can't finish?'

Travis nodded and lifted his arm again. 'Come on, get some sleep. We have a busy day ahead of us tomorrow.'


She had just snuggled in when, out of the corner of his eye, Travis saw something next to his boot. It was something shiny and round and metallic, like a medal of some sort. He wouldn't have seen it at all except the firelight had made it glint in the sand. He reached out to pick it up. It was a large coin. He turned it over and noted the date, still remarkably visible after all those years.

'What is that?' Janey asked him, stirring at his movement and yawning.

'It's what the pirates of the day used to call "a piece of eight", because it was worth eight reales in old Spanish currency.'

'Is it gold?' she asked him, with her eyes shining as he twirled the coin through his fingers.

Travis shook his head. 'No, it's silver.'

'But it's lost pirate treasure, right?'

'Yeah, of course. Here, you have it. Consider it a souvenir from the island.'

'Me? Really? Don't you want to keep it?'

'No, I want you to have it.'

'Oh wow! Thanks. I love it. It's so old. Look, it's dated 1732. That's amazing, but there's got to be lots of pirate treasure still in the Caribbean just waiting to be found, don't you think, Travis?'

'Sure. I have a very good friend who found a great hoard of sunken booty once. It was a while back now, in the 1970s, but he claimed that treasure and he was given a reward for salvaging it. He's a multi-millionaire now. Goes by the name of Booty Bill.'

'Do you think there might be more coins in this cave? Shall we have a hunt about, just in case?'

He laughed. 'No. It's late, and like I said, we're going to have a busy day tomorrow.'

She studied the eight-reales coin for a moment in the light of the fire. 1732 was so long ago, and yet, here it was: a tangible link with the past and a piece of history here in her hand.

She slipped it into her coin purse for safe keeping and then she rested her head on his shoulder.

'Will you tell me a bedtime story about treasure hunting to help me sleep?' she begged. 'Because I'd dearly love to go on a treasure quest. It sounds like the ultimate adventure to me, like in *Treasure Island* by Robert Louis Stevenson. He was from Edinburgh, like me, did you know?'

'Okay, I have a story. And, of course, there are so many stories and legends about treasure buried in the Virgin Islands. I heard this story about a Spanish galleon that was wrecked in these parts during the sixteenth century. Apparently, the crew had all mutinied and two small boats carrying fifty chests each full of silver had set sail for Tortola. One of them reached its destination but the other never arrived. Legend has it that for many years, the Governor of the British Virgin Islands sent officers out to search for it, but the boat and the treasure were never found…'

'*Yo ho ho, it's a pirate's life for me…*' Janey sang softly as she fell fast asleep.


When Janey woke she was alone. In a panic she called out to Travis.

'I'm here,' he replied. 'The sun's just coming up and I'm on lookout.'

Outside, the storm had passed and the sky was clear again. He was using a small rounded rock to grind something against a larger flatter one.

'Preparing breakfast?' she asked him hopefully.

He grinned at her and carried on grinding. He was always preparing something. It was like being castaway with Marco Pierre White. Yesterday he was grinding black peppercorns, although, she had to admit, this time his ingredients didn't look very appetising at all.

'Yuk, it stinks. What is it?' she asked.

'I'm making an explosive,' he explained.

'Arh, I see. Constipated, are you?'

He laughed and then he went on to explain to her how bat guano consisted mostly of potassium nitrate, sometimes called saltpetre, which was one of the three ingredients used in making gunpowder.

'Janey, will you go and fetch me some of the charcoal from last night's fire?

Janey did so. 'Okay, so what's the third ingredient?'

She watched carefully over his shoulder as he finished grinding the bat poop and sprinkled it into a cloth bag he'd made from a piece of his t-shirt.

'Sulphur. Luckily for us, there's lots of it naturally occurring in the ground around here.'

'Lucky, indeed.' Janey looked cautiously at the ground as if it might blow up at any minute.

'Once those three things have been ground into a fine powder, we have to keep it all separate and dry until just before we need to use it.'

She decided not to ask just when he thought that might be.

They waited all morning and well into the afternoon at the cove, and went over the details of their plan to take on the pirates. They talked about distracting them to the beach, disabling the pirate boat with explosives, and then finally taking back *The Mermaid*.

Janey's eyes flashed with both excitement and fear.

'You do know that I've never done anything as adventurous as this in my entire life, don't you?' She thought she'd best warn him of this, just in case he thought she was always running around like a female version of Indiana Jones.

'Then how does it feel being so daring and bold, Janey?'

She felt herself blush. 'It feels good. I feel frightened most of the time, but alive. I feel alive.'

'Well, I couldn't have done any of this without you, although I will admit that I didn't like you at first because I thought you were one of *those* kind of people. You know the ones I mean?'

Janey's face was suddenly glowing like a furnace. Her eyes scanned the coconut shells and explosive powders stacked up in front of them, as if wishing for a distraction from the way this conversation was obviously headed. 'Erm... yes. You mean tourists?'

'Yes. But you are not just a tourist, Janey. You are undoubtedly the bravest woman I have ever met.'

Suddenly she had a huge lump in her throat. So big, that she found it hard to come back with something light and witty to lessen the weight of what he had just said to her.

*The bravest woman I ever met...*


When late afternoon came around, Travis said it was time to put together his hand grenades by mixing and packing his explosive powders into the coconut shells she had collected. Janey helped him by making the fuses out of what was left of his old t-shirt.

Then, while taking it in turns to peer out to sea with the binoculars, the pirate boat suddenly appeared on the horizon. Their wait was over.

They scrambled into position and crawled like commandos on their bellies from their spot on the beach, where they had the dinghy inflated and ready, to the headland, where they could easily see both *The Mermaid* and the approaching pirates.

They counted six of them. All but one of them were small, ugly looking men; these were obviously the crew. They wore military-style pants and boots and black sleeveless vest tops like a uniform of sorts.

They also wore a rack of chains across their chests containing bullets and knives. Their bodies and their bare arms, although scrawny looking, were well defined, with stringy muscles that were decorated with lots of tattoos. They scuttled around the deck of the pirate ship like beetles, gathering their ropes and grappling hooks, while the other pirate, a fearsome-looking beast of a man, oversaw the whole operation.

The pirate captain's body was massive. His limbs were thick, not with fat, but with rippling hard muscles. He reminded Janey of one of those American WWF wrestlers from the TV shows, who had been given a name like *The Destroyer* or *The Bone Crusher* so they would sound as scary as they looked. He had a big long gun strapped to his back as he strode purposefully around on the deck, yelling orders at the others.

Travis and Janey watched and waited from their position, hardly daring to breathe as the pirate boat came alongside *The Mermaid* and the pirates cast their ropes and hooks across to board her.

They were now close enough that they could hear them shouting to each other.

'What are they saying? I can't understand them,' Janey whispered to Travis.

'They're speaking in Creole. Suggesting that the boat's crew, that's us, might be ashore. The men are saying to the captain, the big guy with the rifle on his back, that they should go ashore and look for us. That we might be up to no good.'

'Oh dear. I do hope they don't see our decoy on the beach before they fuel up *The Mermaid*,' Janey whispered. She and Travis then looked at each other in horror and realised their very big mistake.

By setting off later in the day than they had expected yesterday, and getting caught in the storm last night, so not going back to their camp on the beach, they'd forgotten that the decoy rum boxes were still well hidden under the tarpaulin camouflage.

'They won't be able to see them and we need the distraction to get on board *The Mermaid*,' Janey hissed.

'One of us has to go back to uncover the boxes and make sure they see them,' Travis whispered.

'Then I'll go. There is no way I'm staying here with your explosives,' Janey volunteered.

'But, Janey, the waterfall. It is one thing to climb up it but getting down it is another matter.'

Janey hesitated. He was right. How would she ever get down safely, when yesterday they had cut down the overhanging ropes they'd used to abseil down the rock face last time?'

'I'll find a way,' she heard herself saying, while another voice inside her absolutely disagreed.

*You will break your neck, your legs, your arms, and smash your head on the rocks.*

Travis looked at her in concern. 'You'll need to get to the beach as fast as you can. I estimate they'll have her fuelled up and have her ready to go in less than an hour.'

'Yes, I know I can do it. Now, give me your flare gun. Once I have removed the tarpaulin to attract them to the beach, I'll use it to distract the pirates.'

Travis's face was etched with worry. 'Well, as soon as you've fired it, you make sure you get out of there and fast. Janey…?'

She stopped and turned around and looked at him directly. 'Yes?'

'Head out just past the rocks where I went looking for the lobster. I'll come and pick you up once I've taken back *The Mermaid*.'

'You can be sure of it, captain,' she assured him, sticking the gun into her makeshift holster belt.

Janey scuttled back across the cove, keeping her head low as she crossed the beach until she reached the long grasses leading back onto the headland. Once there, she ran as fast as she could until the muscles in her legs cramped and spasmed with pain and she could run no more. She stopped and bent over to catch her breath but, instead, she retched up the boiled crab she'd eaten for lunch. Then she ran on towards the waterfall.

She could hear it before she could actually see it. A low rumbling sound at first and then an uninterrupted deafening roar, as thousands of gallons of water spewed over the giant boulders and spilled downward over the plateau of rocks, not in a single plummet, but in several stages of twisting cascades.

She looked down. It was an incredibly beautiful but terrifying sight. She pondered her death as she hesitated, wondering if her body would ever be found. Then she remembered Travis's words: *'The bravest woman I ever met'*, and she realised that fear was not an option when Travis was relying on her to pull this off. If she didn't get to the beach on time and distract the pirates then they would certainly lose *The Mermaid* and could be trapped on this island for years. Or worse, they could die here; obviously not of starvation with Travis's skills in the food department but of sickness, disease, or eventual madness.

Suddenly she saw a way down. She watched carefully as a plume of water hit a rock to the side of the falls and made its way through a series of what looked like smooth limestone flumes. Her eyes followed the torrent as it twisted and spiralled all the way down into the calm lagoon below.

All the water that had gone before, over many centuries, had softened and carved out the rock face, smoothing it into what effectively appeared to be a water slide. She picked up a chunk of wood and sent it into the flume to study it. She watched it fall and occasionally disappear, only to reappear again below safely and seemingly none the worse for its journey down the falls.

She positioned herself and gathered her thoughts. Then she sat down, edging herself closer and closer to the edge of the rock on her bottom. Her next movement, a slight thrust of the hips, would place her into the torrent of water that would carry her down. She crossed her arms in front of her chest and placed one foot over the other to streamline her shape as much as possible. Then she tipped her body back and slipped into the spiralling flume of white water.

She tried to stay in the fast running slipstream and keep her weight and her head tipped back, trying to protect herself from being forced forward into a dangerous twisting somersault. She kept her eyes closed at this point, as there was no benefit in seeing where she was going. The fact she was going down and going fast was enough for her at that moment. Sometimes she felt herself falling weightlessly through the air. Her tummy lurched and she felt like she couldn't breathe until she hit another flume and then slid along it, all the time gathering momentum, until eventually there was one long falling sensation, and at that point she knew instinctively to take a deep lungful of air and to hold onto it. This was it, the final drop into the lagoon.

She expected to hit the water from a great height and then be carried down into the depths of the lagoon for some way before she could kick her legs and swim up to the surface, but what actually happened wasn't quite as she expected. She became trapped at the bottom of the falls, underwater, in what felt like a washing machine spin cycle.

She splayed her legs and arms and fingers out, trying to grab onto something, anything at all, as it all passed her by. Then she felt her hands and her feet occasionally hitting the sandy bed just beneath her spiralling body. She tried to time it so that she could land on her feet and bounce herself upward. This worked to a point, but she couldn't get enough momentum going to get anywhere near the surface, and she was continually being pushed back down again by the downward torrent and the weight of the water crashing into the lagoon above her.

She tried again and again to bounce herself to the surface and failed.

Rapidly running out of breath, she tried to gather her thoughts and to save the one tiny bit of air that she still had in her lungs. Her panic had now dispersed and her survival instincts had suddenly taken over. Adrenaline was pumping through her veins, reaching her heart and making it beat faster and faster. Meanwhile, her brain began thinking in a calmer and heightened sort of way. Somehow, she knew that she had to change tactic and swim along the bottom of the lagoon in a parallel line, where she could escape the weight of the water above her, and surface in the middle of the lagoon.

When Janey eventually broke the surface of the water, gasping and spluttering and gulping air, she could only think about one thing, and that was getting out of the water and then running as fast as she could to the beach. It was as if her body had switched itself on to autopilot and her mission had become a single thought process.

She had risked her life to get this far and she wasn't going to let anything stop her now.

When she reached the beach she stopped and looked out towards the headland. *The Mermaid* and the pirate boat were still there. She sighed with relief, wiped her sweating brow with the back of her hand, and ran towards their decoy rum boxes. She pulled off the palm branches and hauled away the tent tarpaulin and dragged them into the vegetation at the back of the beach. Then she pulled out the flare gun and pointed it upward. Holding it steady with two hands, she dug her toes into the sand.

She only had one shot, and so she had to do it right. She pulled back on the trigger. It was much stiffer and harder to do than she imagined. There was a loud popping sound and a whoosh as she fired it.

She looked up to see a trail of smoke heading high up into the sky. Then, when she thought it had disappeared or was too high to see, there was suddenly an explosive bang and an enormous plume of orange smoke. The flare was like an enormous firework arcing across the bay.

She looked over at the two boats and in seconds she saw that the pirates were launching an inflatable boat. Only this one had an engine on the back of it, and so it was soon heading in her direction at some speed. She started to run to the end of the beach, to the rocks that Travis had told her to head towards. Once there, she waded into the water waist deep and hid in a recess. She was trembling so violently that what she thought might be the sound of large crabs scuttling over the rocks from their hiding places, was actually the sound of her own teeth chattering.

She could also hear the high pitched sound of the pirates' approaching inflatable boat but was too scared to look out from her hidey-hole, so she crouched down and tried to get her breath back and calm herself out of having a panic attack.

*Maybe they hadn't seen her running toward the rocks?*


Travis watched the beach through his binoculars, willing Janey to get there. His stomach was in knots. He regretted letting her go because she was in real danger at the waterfall. What if she couldn't see a way to get down? What if she fell? He had also watched the pirates fuelling *The Mermaid* and could see they were almost ready to go.

Then, to his joy of joys, he saw Janey on the beach. She was running to the boxes and, smart girl that she was, she was keeping her head down. In a very short time she had the tarpaulin and the palms off and she was drawing her flare gun. He went into a cold sweat at this point because she was holding it aloft but seemed to be having trouble with it.

Then it fired, and that was his signal to move. He dashed to the dinghy, pulled it out from where they had hidden it and floated it onto the sea. He climbed aboard and then he rowed. When he reached the two boats, the pirates were too busy screaming at each other while they lowered their inflatable boat to notice him.

*Shit! They had a motor boat.*

The moment the boat was launched and four of the pirates were headed ashore, he climbed up into *The Mermaid* using the anchor rope. Once on deck, he shimmied over the heavy rope that linked the two boats together and set about laying the charges that would stop their pursuit. He sneaked about, keeping out of sight, until he had set four coconut 'shells' in various susceptible parts of the vessel.

All he had to do now was get back to detach *The Mermaid* before they went off.

He shimmied back across the rope but it was while climbing aboard that he was spotted by the pirate captain, who was still aboard the pirate vessel. He threw a knife, which narrowly missed Travis, lodging itself into the side of the handrail just a fraction away from Travis's head.

Travis glared at him and the pirate glared back. He noticed the pirate didn't have the long rifle on his back any more. He must have handed it over to his shore crew.

'Get him,' the captain yelled to his one remaining crew member on board.

Travis braced himself as a skinny guy, covered in nautical tattoos, launched himself onto the rope between the two boats. He climbed across the gap quickly like a spider scurrying across its web, heading for its kill. Luckily, Travis had the advantage of strength and height and soon had the little guy scooped up and twisted in an arm lock.

'Give up and throw down your weapon!' Travis yelled across to the pirate captain.

The captain drew his hand gun.

'I said, throw it down,' Travis repeated, now standing behind the man he had secured.

But the pirate captain took the shot. It blasted out from the barrel of the gun. The bullet went straight through his crewman, killing him instantly, while clipping Travis on the shoulder.

As both Travis and the dead man hit the deck, all the coconut shells on the pirate boat when off at once in a huge explosion. Travis thought he had been completely deafened by the blast, but then he realised that the dead man had landed on top of him, sheltering him from the worst of the blast and protecting his head from the splinters of wood that were raining through the air. He could hardly believe that the pirate captain had sacrificed the life of his own crew member just to try to fire a bullet into him.

*It was a cold and callous murder.*

His thoughts immediately returned to Janey and the matter in hand. He grabbed his binoculars and searched for her. She was nowhere to be seen but the other four pirates were now on the beach.

He homed in on the sight of them waving their arms and fists in his direction. Their boat was now sinking fast in a blaze of flames and the pirate captain was swimming to shore. Travis wished he could do something about that, but he had to get to Janey, who he assumed would be at the far side of the beach, hiding in the rocks where he'd told her to wait for him.

He quickly gave his boat a quick visual check over. She had some damage, but it was nothing that couldn't be fixed, so he fired up the engine and set off at full speed.

After what may or not have been about five minutes, Janey heard what she assumed to be a gun shot followed by an even louder explosion from the direction of the headland and was compelled to stick her head up and find out what was going on.

*Was Travis all right?*

*Had he managed to place his hand grenades on the pirate ship and take back his boat yet?*

What she saw made her jaw drop. The pirate boat was on fire. There were huge red flames shooting up and licking the sky, together with lots of billowing black smoke.

One of the pirates had jumped overboard and was now swimming for the beach.

*The Mermaid* was thankfully already halfway across the bay, heading towards her and travelling fast. She could see Travis at the helm and so she began waving and yelling, cheering him on.

*Their plan had come together. It had actually worked.*

Unfortunately, the four pirates on the beach had discovered that they'd been tricked and the rum boxes were empty. Then, having seen their boat blown up in front of their own eyes, they were blazing angry. They had heard Janey's shouts and began running along the beach towards her.

She glanced at the approaching *Mermaid* and then back to the pirates; the estimated speed of both giving her a reason to fly into total panic. There was a very real possibility that the pirates would get to her before Travis did. On flailing arms and legs, she started to swim away from the rocks and out to sea, but she'd never been a very good swimmer. She wished she'd been taught the front crawl or the butterfly at all those infernal swimming lessons when she was younger, or at least one style that could push her through the water faster than breaststroke.

She kept her eyes on the approaching *Mermaid* as she swam. It was coming in fast. She could see Travis's face. His eyes were wide and his teeth were clenched as he tried to get everything out of his boat in terms of speed. But Janey was also aware that the pirates were behind her and they were in the water too. She held up her hand to wave to Travis, hoping he would somehow manage to come alongside without slowing down and whip her up out of the water and into his strong safe arms. It was then that she felt a sharp and terrible pain at the top of her head as she was lifted out of the water by her hair and dragged to shore by one of the pirates, who was cursing her with words that she didn't recognise except for one: *bitch.*

She screamed but her high-pitched shrieks were drowned out by the sound of rapid gunfire.

She felt the heat of the hard metal bullets whizzing past her head. Her ear drums felt like they were bursting from the loud crack of shots as they ripped into the side of *The Mermaid*.

At that moment, Janey couldn't tell if she'd been hit or not. All she knew was panic and pain.

The pirate who had dragged her over the rocks to the beach still had a large clump of her blonde hair in his big, filthy, tattooed hand, and the chain of ammunition anchored across his chest was now splashed with her blood from when he'd smashed the side of her face into it. In his other hand he had a rifle, which he now had pointed at Travis's fast disappearing boat.

He spent a moment concentrating on his aim and then he took the shot.

Another pirate was watching the bullet's trajectory using a pair of binoculars. He suddenly cheered, and the two men high-fived each other.

*Had Travis been hit?*

Janey sat quaking on the sand, her body tucked up into a small terrified ball. Through her tears, she could see her arms and legs were cut and bleeding, but her terrified screams had now become silent sobs as she too watched *The Mermaid* speeding away into the distance. If she had been driving that boat, she knew she would be heading back to Antigua at full speed to rally the rescue troops.

*But what if Travis had been shot?*

*What if he couldn't make it?*

*What if he bled out and became unconscious on the way?*

She had to force herself to stop panicking and think positively. If Travis wasn't hit or hurt badly then it would probably take him around three hours to get back and then, if they scrambled a helicopter, it was entirely possible that she could be rescued in around four hours.

She just had to stay alive until then and pray that Travis did too.

# Chapter Nine

One of the pirates pointed his gun at Janey. 'Walk,' he instructed, indicating the direction of the beach. She stumbled to her feet on legs that were shaking so badly it was as if all her supporting muscles were misfiring. She walked in front of him with her hands raised in surrender.

*Please don't shoot me, please don't shoot me, please don't shoot me...* became a mantra on loop in her head and she made her way slowly over to the camp.

'Sit,' ordered the pirate when they got there.

Janey sat, feeling ridiculously grateful for his reprieve.

*Unless, of course, he planned to shoot her while she was sitting down.*

The men then went over to the empty rum boxes and kicked them over angrily.

Janey watched them and feared their retaliation.

*Would they now beat her?*

*Rape her?*

*String her up on a palm tree and then shoot her?*

Until she'd become a castaway on this island, Janey thought she'd known something about fear. Fear of not getting an issue of *Hot Scot* to the printers by deadline day. Fear of speaking in public. Fear of not living up to other people's expectations. Fear of never being truly loved. Fear of never being asked to marry. Only now, when her life was in imminent danger, did she know *real* fear.

Real fear stops you crying when you want to wail your heart out, because you know that tears are a sign of weakness and showing any weakness might get you killed. Real fear paralyses and confuses your senses so, instead of feeling hot and sweaty, you feel shivery and ice cold, and any pain you might be in you are glad of because it is proof you're not actually dead yet. Real fear makes you nauseous yet you know that you can't throw up, because that would be another display of weakness. Janey rammed her fist into her mouth to stop herself retching. When she looked up, the pirates were looking at her curiously.

One took a step forward and held out his hand. 'Give me earrings and the diamond!'

She removed her stud earrings and handed them to him and then she took off her engagement ring. She hated handing over the ring but she knew that Mark would have it insured.

'Money!' he then demanded.

Janey nodded. She had money. A couple of hundred dollars plus the ripped note that Travis had given her back. 'In my bag. It's over there.' She pointed to the small leather bag she'd worn across her body, foolishly thinking they would hand it to her. She watched and groaned as they tipped out the contents. Her makeup, her hair brush, a few toiletries and other paraphernalia including her money purse; it all fell into the sand.

One of the men picked up the money purse and stuck his dirty fingers into it. He sneered at it and threw her cash down, stamping on it with his military-style boot.

'More money!' he yelled angrily.

'We will ask for rich bitch ransom money,' said another of the pirates, waving his gun in the air.

The big ugly pirate captain, the one who had swum ashore from their sinking boat, picked up one of the coins that had fallen into the sand. He twirled it in his fingers and looked at her curiously.

She glared back at him, thinking it might be a good idea to encourage a ransom demand, as being exchanged sounded much better than being shot in the head, and it would also send out a message to Mark and to Travis and to everyone else that she was still alive.

'How much money will you ask for me?' she asked, boldly.

'Twenty-five million US dollars in cash in twenty-four hours, or we will kill you!' yelled the one waving the gun. The others cheered at this, but Janey just managed to stop herself from telling them how ridiculous it was to ask for so much. Not that she didn't think she was worth it, but how could anyone possibly get so much cash together in such a short time? It was impossible.

All she had now to cling to was Travis coming back or she was doomed.

The pirate plan to ransom her off came unstuck as soon as the stupid fools realised they didn't actually have a boat, a radio, or any supplies at their disposal because, thanks to Travis's home-made bombs, they were all now in Davy Jones's locker, at the bottom of the sea.

Janey had to watch them while they got angry all over again. They yelled at each other and swore at her and cursed everything and fired off their bullets into the air. She curled herself up again to make herself as small as possible and covered her head with her hands so that all she could hear was the sound of her own blood thumping through her ears.

When one of the men grabbed her roughly, she fought him off with every ounce of energy left in her body, but it was no use because even the skinniest of them was strong and powerful after years of plundering boats and fighting with people. The others laughed cruelly as she wriggled and struggled against the rope with which he was trying to bind her arms.

*If this was end, then she must die bravely.*

*She must not cry….*

In her struggle, she stamped on something on the sand. She looked down and saw her lipstick and, alongside it, a strip of Mark's anxiety pills.

'Medicine,' she shouted out. 'I need my medicine. Look!' She stretched out her leg and pointed her toe towards the packet. Why on earth she needed anxiety pills in the moments before she was to be hung from a tree was a ridiculous concept, but she was trying to grasp at anything that might delay her last breath being drawn.

'I need my medicine,' she howled.

She was dragged to the nearest tree and pushed against the trunk. The pirate captain went and picked up the pills before he walked menacingly towards her. He emptied several of the pills from the strip into the palm of his hand.

'Tell me why you are on this island and I'll give you your medicine,' he said to her coldly.

'We got stranded here. We were marooned, like castaways.'

'I do not believe you. You are a liar. Tell me the real reason that you came here.'

'No. I'm not lying. You saw for yourself that our boat was out of fuel when you tried to take it.'

In his other hand she saw he had something shiny. She feared it was a blade. *Was he going to slice up her face?* The thought of being cut up made her more afraid that the thought of choking on the end of a noose. He held it up in front of her face and she saw it was a coin like the one Travis had given her. It *was* the one that Travis had given her.

'Where did you get this coin?' he demanded. 'Tell me. It was in your purse.'

Her mind was racing. What should she say? What harm could it do to tell them that she got it from Travis? 'I-I-It was a gift. You know, a souvenir. Travis gave it to me.'

'Travis? Is that the man you are with?'

'Yes, the man you were shooting at on the boat.'

He leaned forward and grabbed her hair. His breath smelled rank. 'And where did he get it?'

Janey squealed in pain but, for some reason unbeknown to her at that time, she thought that telling him the truth might not be a good idea.

'I don't know. He told me it had been in his family for years and years. It was a family keepsake.'

'So then why would he give it to you?'

This was a good question and Janey was running out of good answers.

His grip on her head as she hesitated was getting excruciatingly tighter.

All the pirates were glaring at her, baring their crooked teeth and waiting for her answer. They looked so scary standing there with their military wear and guns and matching tattoos. She noticed they each had the same tribal one of a snake on their necks.

'He paid me with it for… for… for sex!'

Why on earth this explanation was the only thing she could think of was also unbeknown to her at that time. She had just confessed to being a prostitute. The pirates seemed highly amused by this and started laughing. Those who'd understood her English explained the dirty details to those who didn't. The captain jerked back her head and stuffed the pills into her mouth.

The pirates began to light a fire and gather wood and were still jibbing to each other in Creole, while Janey sat thinking. She still had the pills in her mouth and she was considering swallowing them. It would be nice to feel calm and sleepy because it was exhausting being anxious and afraid. The pills would make this whole experience easier to deal with now that the sun was down, especially if they had decided to have some fun with her before they ended her life.

She tried not to sob at being treated so inhumanly, but then spat the pills out onto the sand.

For an hour or more she watched them from her vantage point under her tree, as the men sat around the fire. They were smoking a cigarette and passing it around. From the sweet-scented whiffs coming her way on the breeze, she suspected it wasn't just tobacco. She'd thought them not having any rum might be an advantage for her, but drugged-up pirates was probably much worse.

It had been dark for around half an hour now, which meant it must be around seven o'clock. All being well, Travis wouldn't be too far off reaching Antigua. In just another couple of hours, there was a real chance of her being rescued, and until then she had to remain hopeful, think only positive thoughts, and stay focussed on being the bravest woman that Travis Mathews had ever met.

She looked up at the almost full moon as it rose in the sky and lit up the beach with its silvery light. She thought about Mark and then, to her guilt, realised it was the first time she'd thought of him all day. She tried to justify her lack of thought for him by telling herself that she'd been busy, preoccupied, and concocting a plan to escape the island so that she could return to him and become his wife. And, if all of that had been entirely true, she could have easily been forgiven for not missing him or thinking of him, or for not wondering how he was coping with her being missing for almost four days.

Only she'd spent a large portion of the day thinking about Travis instead, watching him work with his hands, enjoying his conversation and his company and, ever since that kiss, imagining his lips crushing against hers once again. In the cave, she'd slept in his arms with his warm body against hers, listening to the rhythmic beat of his heart, breathing in his masculine smell as it rose up to fill her senses. And to her secret shame, she had dreamt of him making love to her by the campfire light. She had woken up shaken, aroused, and highly disturbed by her sleeping fantasies, wondering how she could possibly dream up such wanton thoughts when she was engaged to be married to another man.

Despite the discomfort of the rope chafing her and the constant sensation of being bitten by ants, she suspected she might have dozed off, because suddenly she was jolted into full consciousness by the sensation of her rope being loosened. Her eyes sprang open and she was about to yell and kick and fight her assailant off when a large hand covered her mouth and a familiar voice whispered into her ear.

'Janey, it's me. Shhh… be quiet.'

'Travis?' she murmured.

'Shhhh…'

It *was* him. It was Travis. She kept her eyes fixed on the men around the fire while he untied her, and she prayed that they wouldn't turn around at that moment and give her their attention.

'Let's go,' he said to her a moment later, in the lightest of whispers.

They crept away together slowly and quietly, hardly daring to breathe until there was enough distance between them and the beach to talk in low voices.

'Did you manage to get back to Antigua? Did you raise the alarm? Did you bring a rescue team?' she asked him in a breathless rattle of words.

'No, I didn't leave. What? Did you actually think that I'd leave you behind? With those men? Why would you even think that, Janey?'

He sounded really annoyed with her for suggesting such an idea.

'Yes. I wanted you to go back to Antigua and get help.'

He took her by the arm and pushed her forward.

'Well, you got help. You got me!'

Janey didn't tell him that he was hurting her arm and that she thought it might be dislocated, she just put one foot in front of the other and let him guide her along through the dense dark jungle.

'Where is *The Mermaid*?' she asked.

'She's moored in a small cove on the other side of the island. It took me two hours to get to you following the coastline, so we must hurry. They are sure to notice you are gone any minute now. We need to get ahead.'

They entered a spot where there was a break in the tree canopy and in the silver moonlight she could see him more clearly. He had a gauze dressing and a bandage wrapped around his upper chest and shoulder area, held in place with duck tape. The dressing was stained with a dark patch of blood.

'Oh no, you are hurt! You need to get to a hospital,' she wailed.

'It's just a flesh wound,' he insisted. 'I found a first-aid kit, so it's fine. Come on, let's keep moving.'

But Janey thought his injuries must be worse than he was telling by the way he was moving and because he'd lost so much blood. 'You know, you really should have gone straight back to Antigua to get that treated. I still can't believe you didn't do that!'

'And I still can't believe that you'd think I'd leave you with those pirates!'

At that moment they heard a crack of gunfire – the pirates had noticed she'd gone.

They tried to increase their pace, but it was difficult to navigate through the undergrowth in the darkness. After another ten minutes or so, breathless and in pain, Janey stumbled on a rock or a root and fell to the ground, twisting her ankle. She kept telling herself to get up and get moving but her body just wouldn't obey. The pain in both her ankle and her shoulder was all consuming.

'I can't get up. I can't go on. You go on without me while you have a chance. They don't know you are here, so let them take me back and you go and get some help.' She felt his arms around her, lifting her up.

'Don't you ever listen to me? I told you that you have already got help. You've got me and I'm not leaving this island without you, Janey.'

As he carried her in his arms, she rested her head against his good shoulder and listened to the sound of his breathing. She was aware of his heat, his sweat, and his sticky blood soaking through his dressing and through her shirt. She could hear the sound of the sea crashing against rocks but then, after a little while, she heard nothing more.

When she woke, she was still leaning against his chest. His heart was beating slower now and his breathing was deeper and rhythmic. She opened her eyes and blinked against complete darkness. She could see nothing at all.

*Was it still night? Where was the moon, or the stars at least?*

She moved her legs and a searing pain shot right through her. 'Ooh! Wow, that hurt! I think I've broken my ankle.'

'Here, let me strap it for you. I didn't want to wake you up but it really needs attention.'

Travis flicked on a small torch and held it in his teeth as he moved to tend to her foot. He used a couple of sticks as splints and strips of vegetation as bindings.

She gritted her teeth as he worked. 'Where are we now and how long was I out?'

'We are in a cave very close to the cove where I left the boat. You've been out for a couple of hours.'

'And you carried me here?' A rhetorical question because how else would she have got here?

He laughed. 'Yeah. You know, Janey, you really should eat more. You're as light as a feather.'

She looked up at his face and then back to his big hands as they cupped her swollen ankle and then gasped, not with anxiety or relief or fear or pain, but from a feeling of warmth that had started in his smile and travelled with his hand through her body and down to her foot.

'I don't think your ankle's broken but it is badly sprained. Are you hurting anywhere else? Did they hurt you?' He used his torch to check her over as if he was doing a quick body scan.

'My right shoulder hurts. I think it's dislocated,' she explained, feeling badly even mentioning it when he had a bullet lodged in his own.

He gently explored her shoulder and then he looked right into her tear-filled eyes.

'I can fix it, but it's gonna hurt like hell and you can't scream.'

She laughed nervously. 'Oh, so you're a doctor now, as well as a captain and a chef?'

'No, but I had this happen to me once, so I know how it's fixed. You trust me?'

*Yes, she trusted him. With all her heart. He came back for her. He said he wouldn't leave without her.*

She nodded and braced herself as he held her hand and pulled her arm sharply upwards.

When Janey regained consciousness, there was a glimmer of new daylight streaming into their cave. Travis was watching her intently. He smiled as she opened her eyes.

'Feeling better?'

She rotated her shoulder and rubbed it with her left hand. It was bruised but the really bad pain had gone and she could certainly use it again.

'Yes, I think I'd add miracle worker to my résumé, if I were you, Travis.'

'Great. So, are you ready to move, because I thought we'd skip breakfast this morning?'

She nodded. 'Yes. I'm ready for anything.'

She got to her feet. With the binding supporting her ankle, she could put her weight on it.

'We have to get down to the cove without the pirates seeing us,' he told her.

'What? Are they outside?' Her voice trembled at the thought.

'No, but they are close by and it's not going to be easy to get across the beach without being seen.' He helped her to hobble to the cave entrance and they both peeped outside.

Janey sniffed the air. 'Wood smoke?'

'Yeah, they camped just behind the tree line last night. We have to assume they are still there.'

The tree line was directly between them and the beach.

'I moored *The Mermaid* in a tight ingress just around the cove,' Travis told her. 'She can't be easily seen, so I hope that keeps her safe from the pirates, for a while anyway.'

'We'll have to find a way to get to her without crossing the beach or scaling the headland, because even without our injuries, that looks impossibly steep,' Janey noted.

'The only way is to skirt around their camp and make our way through the jungle.'

'What about this cave?' Janey queried, glancing behind them back into the cavern where they'd just spent the night. 'Do we know how deep it goes and if there is another exit further back?'

Travis kissed her forehead quickly. 'Good thinking. Let's go and explore.'

Once back inside the inky-black damp space, he switched on his torch and Janey followed him closely.

They felt their way along the rock and soon discovered a jagged vertical slice in the cave's belly, which looked like it could be a passageway. They slipped inside it, moving slowly and carefully as it became even narrower. Janey prayed that they didn't get stuck because there wasn't even enough space to turn around in.

'This island is a honeycomb of caves, so let's hope this one isn't a dead end,' he commented.

And every time Travis thought that they had come to a dead end, and her heart sank at the thought of having to retrace their steps in reverse, they'd find that the passageway did a sharp right or left, forming a new route. Sometimes, there were two paths to choose from and no way of knowing which might lead to freedom or which would trap them forever in this dark slimy cave. Janey held on to the waistband at the back of Travis's shorts as they moved through the darkness.

'Why don't we go left and right alternatively?' she suggested. 'Then we might end up going in something of a straight line rather than going round in circles?'

They continued on, following the damp walls and the beam of the torch, which Janey thought was getting dimmer. She didn't want to ask if Travis had any spare batteries on him because she suspected that the answer to that would be no.

They might have travelled for about half a mile, it was hard to know, but if they didn't find another exit to the cave system soon it was going to be a very difficult and dark return journey.

'Are we getting anywhere?' Janey asked him. Her ankle was throbbing again and she was feeling more and more claustrophobic. She'd also just grazed her hip quite badly.

Suddenly they stopped moving forward.

'Janey, I'm gonna switch off the torch. I see something ahead, but I can't tell if it's just a reflection bouncing off the wet wall back at us.'

They both stood still as he plunged them into total darkness. Janey held her breath but then, as her eyes adjusted, peeping under Travis's arm, she could definitely see a shaft of light. It came from a narrow crack ahead of them.

'Yes, look. It's a way out!' she yelled.

'It looks a bit tight. Let's hope we can fit through it,' Travis replied.

He inhaled sharply and then squeezed himself through, snagging and losing the bandage that had been holding his dressing together. Janey slipped through the gap more easily, being smaller, and then, once through into the diffused light of the jungle, she saw for the first time the small bloody hole in his chest in which the bullet was still lodged.

Instinctively, she wanted to turn away, but she forced herself to look again at his wound. It needed tending to but they had nothing at their disposal. The bullet hole was leaking with a steady stream of blood and it was already attracting flies.

'We have to do something to try to stop the bleeding. Can I use your knife please?'

He took a penknife from the back pocket of his shorts and handed it to her warily.

Janey removed her vest top. His eyes immediately dropped to her lace-cup bra, through which her small pert breasts were clearly visible. To her embarrassment, her nipples stiffened under his gaze. She began to cut the fabric of the vest lengthways to make strips that she could tie together to make a makeshift bandage. She worked quickly, wrapping the cotton fabric around him and packing the wound with flat waxy leaves. He gasped in pain as she pulled it tight and made a knot.

Afterwards they didn't speak. They just sat on the rocky plateau that was eye level with the tree canopy for a while, like Tarzan and Jane, looked down at the jungle floor below them and wondered how to get down there.

Janey sighed with relief at being able to take the weight off her throbbing ankle. Despite their newly precarious position, it seemed enough to be outside and able to breathe warm humid air.

Travis thought about how much blood he had lost so far from his bullet wound and how it hadn't helped his damaged shoulder having to dig a grave in the sand for the pirate crewman who had been shot on his boat but he'd had no choice but to do so. He decided not to mention this gruesome job to Janey just yet and reached out to the nearest palm frond with his good arm and gave it a good shake.

A coconut was duly despatched to the ground.

They both watched it fall and then smash on impact.

Janey groaned. 'How on earth will we get down?'

'I reckon we're gonna have to use the tree to climb down.'

All the trees around them were tall palms that looked so very pretty, swaying in the tropical breeze, but with their tall ribbed trunks there was nothing to hold on to. It looked impossible.

'How?'

'We'd have to make some kind of body sling, like the coconut gatherers do.'

She turned to see if he was serious and saw that he was staring at her nipples again, then he grinned in a way that involved his eyebrows being wiggled.

She gasped. 'No way! There is *no way* you are getting my bra off to use as some kind of sling.'

Still grinning, he indicated to the vegetation hanging off the underside of the ledge they were sitting on. 'Actually, I was thinking we could utilise those vines. You know, like we did when we climbed down the waterfall?'

It took them around an hour to twist and knot the vines into three long ropes. Then, using one of them, Travis managed to lasso the nearest palm tree.

Janey was super impressed when he roped the tree on his first attempt and then anchored it firmly to a rock.

He told her that acquiring rope skills had been a necessary part of growing up in Texas, for which she was entirely grateful, knowing that if either the rope or the knots gave way while they were making their precarious crossing, they would be catapulted into the air like circus performers.

He attached the second rope to Janey, wrapping it many times around her waist, until she looked like she'd been captured by boa constrictor. Then he attached the third rope to himself in the same way. Travis climbed carefully from the ledge onto the tree, holding onto the palm fronds, until he could find a firm point to anchor the other end of his rope.

Janey watched his technique carefully and fretfully, terrified for her turn.

As he lowered himself through the palm canopy there was a cracking sound. Janey's hand leapt to her mouth to stifle a scream, as for a brief moment, she believed he'd fallen. But then she saw him twirling gracefully at what was a reasonably controlled pace around the trunk of the tree, as the rope unwound itself from around his waist and lowered him to the ground.

When he got down, she cheered.

He shouted up to her. 'Okay, so that's how it's done. Now it's your turn.'

Janey was just about to make her move when the five pirates appeared from the tall jungle undergrowth below her and surrounded Travis. He drew his knife and waved it at them but a small knife was no defence against their big guns. She watched in horror as, defeated, he plunged the knife into the trunk of a tree and then held up his hands in surrender.

The biggest and ugliest pirate, the captain, looked up at Janey and leered at her as she stood helplessly on the ledge.

'You. Come down!' he yelled.

'No!' Travis ordered. 'Janey. Go back in the cave. Quickly.'

As the pirate aimed his gun up at her, Janey did as Travis ordered and slipped back into the cold darkness of the cave. Once inside, however, knowing she didn't have a torch and that she was on her own, she stopped and allowed herself a moment to think rationally about her next move.

She decided to wait, hoping they might believe she had run deep into the cave to make her own escape. Then once they'd moved on, she could swing down the tree as Travis had demonstrated and follow them. There was no way she could leave him. She had to rescue him before he bled to death.

After what seemed a long time, she found the courage to go outside again and to peer down from the open ledge to check if they were gone. When she saw that they had, she started to panic.

*How long had they been gone?*

*Where had they gone?*

*And what did they intend on doing with Travis?*

The pirates used the vine rope still attached to Travis to lead him through the jungle as their captive. They showed him no mercy nor made any allowances for his injuries, dragging him along, and occasionally jabbing him in the shoulder with the butt of a rifle. He'd almost blacked out with the pain several times, but knew that he must stay conscious, so he could tell the direction in which they were heading. Right now they were headed south-east, which he could tell from the position of the sun in the sky, but there seemed little point in asking where they were going, as no doubt he would find out soon enough. He worried about Janey. Had she got lost inside the cave? He hoped that she'd had the good sense to wait there a while and then to climb down the tree, so that she could get back to *The Mermaid* and get them some help.

*Had he told her where she was moored?*

*Yes, he remembered doing so, but could she steer her way out of the tight spot he'd left her in?*

*Of course she could, she was as smart as she was beautiful.*

Eventually, they came out of the jungle and onto a pebble beach. He realised they'd reached the other side of the island, the wilder side, where the waves were huge and crashed dangerously against the rocks. They were moving toward a large dark opening in the headland. It was yet another cave. He kept looking around and watching for opportunities to escape but, so far, there hadn't been any.

Inside this particular cave, to his surprise, there was a large area of bright daylight. Above, in the roof of the cave, there was a huge hole letting in this light. It was an opening commonly known as a blow hole or what had been a blow hole once: a natural erosion in the rock caused by the incoming tides over many thousands of years. There was also a large pool of water directly under the blow hole, which was being fed by water falling through a gash in the rock face. Around the walls of the cave there were elevated layers of natural ledges in the rock. These ledges were stacked with boxes and pallets and all sorts of stuff; pirate booty no doubt, where the water couldn't reach it at high tide. From the layout inside this cave, this was quite clearly Pirate HQ.

Travis was hit violently on the shoulder with the blunt butt of the gun again. The searing pain sent him to his knees. He fell forward into the pool of water, which he sucked at greedily as soon as he tasted sweet fresh water in his mouth. The pirate then pulled him upright by his hair and, although he fought hard to stay conscious and to save himself, it was no use and his eyes closed as he spiralled into darkness.

Janey eventually reached the ground. She did so nowhere near as gracefully as Travis had done, as she'd managed to get herself firmly stuck half-way, and had feared that she would be there until she died of thirst or starvation which, she calculated, might be mercifully sooner rather than later.

However, through luck or desperation, she had somehow freed herself by unknotting the right knots and now she'd made it down at last. She hid the vine rope in the undergrowth, as it was too heavy for her to consider carrying it on the chance that she'd need to use it again, and then she limped through the jungle as fast as could be considered hot-pursuit, following a track of muddy footprints.

The trail led to a beach. If it had been a sand beach it would have made the tracking easier, but it was made up of large round pebbles instead. She sat down at the edge of the tree line, hiding behind foliage, while considering the way some of the pebbles on the beach had been disturbed. It looked, in some parts, as if something quite heavy had been dragged across it and she feared that something was likely to be an unconscious Travis.

She had been tracking splashes of blood along the way too, which meant he was bleeding again.

She knew she didn't have much time because he didn't have much time, so she stood and then immediately sat down again. There was a man, one of the pirates, standing over there on the rocks and he had a gun. At least she knew now where she would find Travis.


No one had been more surprised to find themselves alive than Travis when he woke up. He was tied to an old mooring post and his shoulders had been pulled back to keep him restrained tightly against the wood. He groaned with pain. He couldn't stop himself. The water, red with his blood and lapping waist deep against his body, seemed to be rising fast.

The pirate captain, who was standing on one of the elevated ledges nearby, heard him moan.

'Good…,' he said, 'you are awake, just in time to answer my questions.'

Travis shook his head. There was no way he was going to tell him where he'd left the boat.

'You can go to hell, or I will, before I'll tell you anything.'

'Tell me where you found this coin.'

Travis looked up at him in astonishment. 'What coin?'

'Don't lie! Tell me where you found it and perhaps I'll untie you.' The pirate captain checked the time. 'You have just twelve minutes before high tide.'

Travis felt a surge of blood pumping out of his wound, accelerated by his rapidly beating heart.

That was *his* watch on the pirate's wrist: the watch his father had given him on his twenty-first birthday. He struggled against the ties binding him. If only he could break free and get hold of this thieving pirate bastard… but it was impossible.

The pirate held up a coin between his index finger and thumb so that Travis could see it.

'Your woman, she had this coin on her and she said you gave it to her. Where did you find it?'

Travis started laughing.

*So that's what this was all about. The pirate actually thought he knew were the treasure was, the famous 1732 lost silver reales.*

'I've never seen it before. What is it?' he asked innocently.

'You know exactly what it is. This coin is one of the missing hoard. Where did you find it?'

Travis looked directly into the eyes of his captive. He knew that even if he told him, that this piece of shit would never keep to his bargain and untie him, and he was damned if he'd stoop so low to beg to this low-life thieving bastard, who was wearing *his* watch, in order to save his life.

*No. He'd rather die.*

Travis's silence had sealed his fate as far as the pirate captain was concerned.

He flipped the coin into the blood-stained water and it landed at Travis's feet.

Travis saw it settle itself into the sand. That would be the way he would settle too, no doubt, as the water rushing into the cave was now up past his shoulders. He thought of his past, he thought of what the future might have been for him. He thought about Janey, and reluctantly resigned himself to his watery grave.


Janey watched and waited from her vantage point for the right time to make her move. The pirate guarding the entrance to the cave had now been joined by another. She watched as they had an animated conversation, shouting at each other and waving their guns. Then the others came out too; Travis wasn't with them. Then they all began walking into the jungle again, and once they were out of sight, she hurried towards the cave as stealthily as she could.

Inside, she could hear the roar of water. She hesitated for a second before going on but then made her way through a dark passage that led into a big open cavern. It was lit with natural light from a large round hole in the ceiling, which beamed sunlight straight down into a round pool of blue water. A tiny rainbow had formed in the mist from the waterfall feeding it. It really was spectacularly beautiful.

Then she saw him. He was tied to a post and up to his neck in water. His head was slumped forward and he was gasping for breath. She assessed the situation quickly. It was almost high tide and the base of the cave would soon be flooded. He had just minutes before he drowned.

She raced forward and jumped into the pool. When she reached him, she tipped his head back and said, 'Travis, it's me. I'm going to get you out of here.'

She worked quickly to try to untie him but the vine bindings were really tight and the knots he had expertly tied wouldn't budge. He suddenly gave out a long groan and then a choked gurgling sound as his head fell forward again into the rising water. She began to panic.

There was no way to untie him in time. She needed a knife.

Then she suddenly remembered. Oh joy of joys! She had pulled Travis's penknife out of the tree after climbing down from the ledge. She felt inside the pocket of her shorts and, much to her relief, it was still there. She flicked the blade open and took a gulp of air before going under the water to see how best to cut through the vines.

She rubbed the blade of the knife against the rubbery bindings and cutting through them seemed to take forever. She had to come to the surface for air three times in total, and when she finally got him freed, Travis's face was underwater and he wasn't breathing any more.

She dragged his dead weight to the side of the pool, crying and shouting his name, begging him to stay with her. Then she began pumping his chest, thumping at his heart and getting covered in splatters of his blood from his wound. She looked at his face. He looked so handsome even in death.

His eyes were closed but his lips were slightly parted, so nervously she leaned down to attempt to give him the kiss of life. She'd never had to do this before but she had an idea how it was done.

His lips felt full and soft and slightly salty under hers when she took a deep breath and pressed her lips firmly onto his, sealing their mouths together.

But then, to her alarm, his lips began to move against hers, deepening the kiss, and then she felt his tongue come into play.

*What the...?*

She pulled away from him to see that his eyes were open wide and they were laughing at her.

'The things a guy has to do to get a kiss these days…' he drawled.

'You bastard! I thought you were dead. That's so not fair!' she gasped, rubbing her mouth with the back of her hand.

She didn't know whether to slap him or sob with relief.

'Oh, Travis, you really had me worried that time. I thought you'd gone and left me.'

'No way. I told you I wouldn't leave you, Janey.'

He was coughing hard now and spitting out water.

'You were under the water such a long time. It took me so long to cut the vines,' she exclaimed.

'I used my free diving technique. I saturated my body with oxygen before I went under and it gave me another couple of minutes.'

For someone who had almost died, he seemed mighty pleased with himself.

While he was recovering, Janey took a look around. There was a lot of stuff being stored in this cave on ledges all around them. There was a series of wooden ladders giving access to the higher parts of the cavern, which were also stacked high with various goods, no doubt from boats, yachts, and any other type of vessel that the pirates had plundered. She noticed cases of champagne, boxes of jewellery, and what looked like other valuable merchandise. On the nearest ledge, her eyes settled on a macramé box that looked familiar. She went to it and smiled. It was the box that had been taken from Travis's boat. When she turned to show him it, he was back on his feet.

He gave her a broad smile at seeing the box and ran his finger over the pattern in the wood.

'Now I know where it is, it would be better to leave it. We have to get back to *The Mermaid* as fast as we can, because you don't need me to tell you what will happen if the pirates get to her first.'

She nodded in agreement. 'Do they know where she's moored?'

'No, but that's not to say they won't find her. They seem to know this island pretty well.'

'But can we make it? They have a good start over us.'

'Yeah, I have an idea for a shortcut.'


Mark sat at a desk in his suite at the hotel staring at the blank piece of paper in front of him. He was trying to think of something poignant to say in his eulogy about his relationship with a woman who would have taken his name by now if she hadn't been so cruelly snatched away from him by fate. *His stolen dreams.* Perhaps he could start with that? He could hardly mention the last time he and Janey had seen and spoken to each other, because they had been arguing. She had been disappointed in him for not joining her on her doomed trip.

*If only she'd listened to him instead of being so stubborn, she would still be alive.*

*If he'd gone with her, as she had wanted him to, then he would be dead too.*

Perhaps he could talk about that: *His lucky escape*?

Maybe he was suffering from survivor's guilt?

Yes, of course, that was why he felt so bad, so very guilty. It was an actual condition, something he'd heard about in those who'd had lucky escapes.

Not that he would describe himself as being lucky.

Not at all. If anything, he'd been very unlucky indeed.


They stood together right on the edge of the point, a sheer cliff face looking down at the dark blue water below. To their left, far below, was a long stretch of coastline and a narrow white sand beach, and to the right was a small cove where *The Mermaid* was bobbing up and down on the water.

'Are you sure there is no other way?' Janey pleaded.

'Not if we want to get to her first. There are no rocks below. I saw that when I brought the boat in,' he assured her, 'and you can tell how deep it is here just by the darkness of the water. This is not going to kill us, I promise.'

'Okay. Let's go on the count of three…' said Janey, taking a deep breath and a step forward.

She was feeling utterly terrified, as throwing herself down a waterfall now seemed like child's play compared to throwing herself off such a high cliff into the sea.

Travis grabbed her trembling hand tightly and they started counting together.

'Ready? One... two...'

'No, stop!' she yelled, turning to face him. 'I think there is a good chance that this will kill us, Travis. So before we do this, I want to do this...'

She pressed her lips hard against his and he responded by kissing her as passionately. Their mouths moved together quite desperately, their tongues touched and their breathing became as erratic as their beating hearts.

Travis wrapped his good arm around her and pulled her to him even tighter, literally whisking her off her feet, and then in one swift movement, he took them both off the edge of the cliff.

# Chapter Ten

Janey came up coughing and spluttering for air. After falling from such a great height, she had plunged deeply into the sea, so far down that she thought she would never find her way back to the surface. She looked around for Travis.

A moment later he popped up beside her, immediately yelling, 'We made it!' as if he hadn't really expected them to survive after all.

They swam over to *The Mermaid* and Travis tried to use the anchor rope to haul himself onto the deck but, with his shoulder bleeding heavily, he just couldn't manage it. Janey climbed up instead, ignoring her sprained ankle and her bruised shoulder, and tossed down the rope ladder for him.

He climbed up unsteadily, weak from losing so much blood, but insisting they waste no time in making their escape. She held out her hand to help him with his final step onto the boat.

He took her hand, and once on board he pulled her close to him again.

She wrapped her arms around his neck and looked into his eyes. He looked deeply into hers, smiling and his lower lip quivering. He pressed his forehead against hers and sighed. There was no need for either of them to say anything. Two people didn't go through something like they'd just been through without forming a special kind of empathy, so they simply stood there for a moment, enjoying that they were still alive and that they were together.

When they were done with their moment, they immediately launched into action.

Janey pulled up the ladder and cranked up the anchor. On her signal, Travis started the boat's engine and it roared into life. As they prepared to set off they could see the pirates running along the beach.

'Janey, get down!' Travis insisted. 'Their pistol fire won't reach us but they have a rifle, so keep your head down.'

The boat made a turn and then they made their escape at full speed and in a hail of gunfire.

Only when they were out at sea at a safe distance away from the island, did Travis pull back on the throttle a little. Only then did they allow themselves to actually believe they had secured *The Mermaid* and escaped both the pirates and the island.

Travis called her over to him and she went and stood behind him at the helm. He was trembling and he looked as white as a ghost.

She put her arms around his waist and pressed her wet body gently against his. 'You are cold. I need to get you warm.'

'Have you ever driven a boat, Janey?' he asked her.

'Nope, but I can drive a car and they both have a steering wheel, so it can't be too hard.'

'Boats are nothing like cars. When you are drive a car you don't have to take into account things like cross currents and wind conditions, so I'll need to show you the basics. There's a chance I'll lose consciousness and, if I do, it will be up to you to get us back to Antigua in one piece.'

'Oh! Really? Are you serious? Me drive the boat, without you to help me?'

Travis started to tell her why it was important to hit the swell of the bigger waves out at an angle, so that they didn't cause a rough ride or damage the boat. She stood at the helm on her tiptoes, just slightly too short to have a good view out of the window that was continually being dashed with white spray. Gripping the steering wheel, she tentatively took the controls. Travis stood behind her, encouraging her to keep true and to stay steady. He then told her how to stay on course for Antigua.

'As we head back, you'll notice there are lots of other islands, islets and rocks on both sides so you will have to stay in the clear channel. Think of it as staying on the road. You'll also see lots of buoys in various colours, but it's the green and the red ones that are important. These are the road markers.'

Janey considered the navigation to be the hardest part and she tried to concentrate.

'You must remember to keep the red buoys on your right as you return. Okay?'

Janey nodded and tried to memorise his instructions.

*Red. Right. Return.*

On the beach in Antigua, in Janey and Travis's memory, a lone piper played a mournful tune on the bagpipes while everyone wept. Mark was inconsolable, as was Gwen, who fanned herself with a copy of *Hot Scot Magazine* as she sobbed hysterically.

Janey's mum and dad, Flora and Douglas, had flown in that morning on a British Airways flight and they now stood side by side, stoically dignified, under the shade of the marquee that had been erected to protect the privacy of the mourners from other guests, who had gathered, some purely inquisitively, to pay their respects.

'Janey was our only child…' they explained to those who came to offer their condolences.

Travis's parents stood with Travis's estranged American ex-wife, Madison, who wore a large black hat with a veil covering her face to great effect.

'This is no time for any acrimony between us,' his parents told everyone, just to make clear that except for today, they still hated this woman for cheating on their son.

To counter their rudeness, Madison introduced herself to everyone as 'the grieving widow'.

Travis's best friend, who went by the name of Booty Bill, stood a respectable distance away from them all and kept looking down to re-read and memorise the eulogy he was preparing to give.

A barefoot minister arrived to stand on the waterline. He held a bible in one hand and the other he held high in the air to give blessings. Mark chose this moment to collapse into the sand in front of him.

'Please get this poor man some medical attention,' the Minister instructed.

Leo, the hotel manager, got Mark to his feet and ordered him another drink from the bar.

On board *The Mermaid*, Janey was concentrating hard on steering the boat. She'd missed coming into the marina because a large yacht had been in her path. So instead, she headed off around the bay and towards the beach. If she could stop the boat in the middle of the bay, where lots of people swam and played in the water, she could call for help.

Travis had spent the last hour unconscious and she was terrified he would die.

She kept yelling at him to stay with her, to stay awake and talk to her, while she drove the boat as fast as she dared. 'Tell me more about your dad? I remember you mentioned him to me once at the cave, when the lightning struck?' She kept talking because she didn't know what else to do.

She had to save him. They'd only been together a few days, but in that time she'd almost become a different person. Travis was important to her. He had saved her life and she had saved his. They were forever connected because of that fact. How many people could actually say that? Not many.

As she came around the headland and entered the bay, she could see the familiar hotel buildings with their palm-thatched roofs in front of her. She cried with relief. There were people on the beach.

'We made it, Travis! We are here. In just a couple of minutes we will have help.'

She sounded the horn several times. It came blasting out as a deep drone that no one could miss.

Janey stopped the engine, cast the anchor and then rushed to Travis's side. He was out cold. His lips were blue. She lay on the deck with him and pressed her body to his, trying to warm him. She kissed his lips and stroked his head and kept asking him over and over again to stay with her.

*Please don't die, please don't die, please don't die....*


With the reading of the eulogies over, the Minister said the final prayers and the congregation stood with their heads lowered and said 'Amen'.

Everyone took a moment to consider the sadness and loss of these two fine young people. In that moment of silence, the intrusive sound of a boat's engine made the Minister glare at Leo. Hadn't he insisted that water sports in this cove be banned during the time of the service?

Then Honey gasped and she began pointing and screaming. 'It's Travis. It's *The Mermaid*. Look everyone, look!'

Indeed it was *The Mermaid* and she sounded her horn several times and then stopped dead in the water. There was a frantic scramble from the beach as some swam out and some took canoes.

Leo got on his phone to call the coastguard.

Honey led the swimmers while Mark, who couldn't swim, waited helplessly on the beach.

# Chapter Eleven

They were taken straight from the beach to the hospital by coastguard helicopter. In the emergency room, Janey was given X-rays to check on her ankle sprain and her shoulder dislocation, while Travis was rushed straight into the operating theatre to have his gunshot wound treated.

This all felt like a dream to her; an out of body experience. Janey couldn't quite believe she was back in the real world. She sat quietly while everyone dashed about attending to her scrapes. A nurse sutured her cuts. Someone made her a cup of hot sweet tea but she found she could hardly hold the cup because she was shaking so badly. Another nurse helped her get it to her mouth.

A doctor came over to see her. 'It seems you are experiencing delayed shock, Miss Sinclair. Quite normal after what you've been through. Otherwise, you are in good shape all considering, and there shouldn't be any lasting damage. I'm going to release you into the care of your family who will take you back to your hotel for some rest and recuperation.'

Janey told him she was not going anywhere until she knew that Travis was going to be okay.

While she waited, two police detectives arrived and asked if she was able to offer them a statement. Her doctor advised against it, but Janey insisted that she was ready and willing.

So she told them about the boat's engine stopping about halfway to Tortola and them being marooned and castaway on the island. How they were robbed and kidnapped and shot at by the pirates who were using the island as a hideout for their loot. She told them how she and Travis had managed to reclaim *The Mermaid* and how, in the process, the pirate's boat had been sunk. 'So you see, with no boat, those pirates are still trapped on the island!'

The detectives immediately sent word to the coastguard to scramble a taskforce.

'Can you identify the man who shot Captain Travis Mathews?' she was asked.

Janey began to tremble even more at the memory of the awful moment when the rifle had been fired at Travis while he was fleeing on the boat.

'Yes, I c-c-can.'

'I think that's enough for now,' the doctor insisted. 'Miss Sinclair needs to rest.'

The detectives thanked her for her cooperation and backed off, informing the doctor that they needed to interview Travis too, and that getting a statement from him was a priority.

'And that will be when Mr Mathews had fully recovered from his surgery.'

'How is he?' Janey begged, suddenly seeing a nurse emerge from the operating room.

'He's doing fine. The bullet has been removed, but he'd lost a lot of blood so he needed a transfusion.

He's lucky that you managed to get him here in time to save his life.'

She tried not to sob with relief. 'When can I see him?'

At that moment, there was a commotion and Mark came rushing into the emergency ward. He dashed over to hug her tightly.

'Oh, Janey, I thought I'd never see you again!'

She winced under the power of his squeeze, and was surprised to find he smelled very strongly of alcohol rather than his usual lime cologne. Following in his wake were her mother and father, who too looked incredibly relieved to see her.

Then an older couple and a younger woman arrived. Everyone was dressed for a funeral. It was really rather disconcerting.

'We've just been told that we can take you back to the hotel,' her father told her.

Janey immediately objected. 'No, we can't go yet. We have to stay a bit longer.'

'It's okay, darling. The doctor has given you the all clear,' her mother insisted.

'No, Mum, it's not okay. I need to see Travis.'

At that moment, Travis came out of the operating theatre on a trolley, pushed along by a posse of nursing staff. He was covered with a green sheet but Janey could see a bare arm with drips going into it. Several bags of liquid on a tall stand were being wheeled alongside him by another attendant. Janey leapt to her feet, pushing Mark aside to get to Travis's side.

'Travis, it's Janey! I've been so worried about you, but they say you are going to be okay.'

His eyes flickered open at the sound of her voice but he was barely out of his induced sleep.

The attendants kept the bed moving forward and soon Janey was left behind.

'I'll come back and see you later…' she called out, as he disappeared into a side room.

'Darling, for goodness sake, let the poor man recover before you start pestering him,' Mark insisted, using his condescending barrister-in-court tone with her.

'Let's get you back to the hotel,' said her mother. 'You look like you need a nice hot bath and some clean clothes.'

Janey looked down at herself to see that she was wearing a stranger's t-shirt, which had been hastily and generously given to her on the beach to cover her modesty, because she had used her shorts to try to pack Travis's wound again, and had arrived back in only her torn, muddy and bloodied underwear. Something that hadn't escaped Mark, whose first words upon being reunited with her on the beach had been not 'Janey, darling, you are alive' but 'Janey, darling, where are your clothes?'

She nodded to her mother. A bath sounded truly wonderful. Now that she knew Travis was going to be okay, she could always come back and see him later, when she was clean and fresh and he'd had a chance to regain consciousness. She needed to ask him something. Something very important.

When Travis heard Janey's voice, he'd tried to open his eyes but his lids were heavy and the ceiling lights above him were blinding. Blurry images swam before him and he had desperately tried to blink them away so that he could see her. But when his vision momentarily cleared, it wasn't Janey he saw but a well-dressed, dark-haired man speaking in a very deep and pronounced Scottish accent.

*'Darling, for goodness sake, let the poor man recover...'*

In those brief and woozy seconds, Travis had taken measure of the man who was obviously Janey's fiancé. He looked just as rich, stylish and slick, as he had feared. He had caught a glimpse of an expensive watch his wrist and a gold nugget of a ring on his finger as he lifted his arm to guide Janey away from him.

Travis wasn't used to feeling intimidated, but what had he been thinking?

What had made him think he had a chance with a woman like Janey once they got back here?

He had nothing to offer her. His boat was weather-beaten. His equipment was on its last sea legs and, if he was honest, so was he. His business had been slow since the world-wide recession because all the tourists that came to the islands were watching every damn dollar.

Even his house on the beach had a roof that leaked when it rained.

He couldn't ever see a woman like Janey living somewhere like that.

No, now they were back to reality, he had to accept that whatever he and Janey had while they were on that island together had not been real and it certainly didn't apply to real life.

He woke sometime later to find he was being made comfortable by a nurse, who then checked his drip lines. He saw two men hovering in the doorway.

'I'm sorry, but you gentlemen will have to come back later,' the nurse told the two men.

'What do they want?' Travis asked, trying to stay focussed while the room was spinning.

'They need a statement from you, but there'll be plenty of time for that after breakfast.'

Travis closed his eyes. The room was spinning again. When he woke sometime later, the nurse was back.

'Are you in any pain?'

He said not. He said he felt much better and he asked how soon he could go home.

She plumped his pillows and encouraged him to sit up a little. 'Not until you've eaten all your dinner,' was the reply.

'Then I'll have a rib-eye steak, medium-rare with fries on the side, please.'

She laughed. 'Oh, I'm glad someone's feeling better!'

When his minced beef and mashed potatoes arrived, he ate it all anyway and even polished off his vanilla custard dessert.

After his dinner plates were cleared, he used the remote control to switch through the TV channels. He settled on a news channel. It was showing a clip of the five pirates in handcuffs being taken off a coastguard boat. He gave out a loud cheer.

Moments later, he was agreeing to give the police his statement.

He told them how his boat had stalled on their way to Tortola due to an engine problem. He preferred to call it an engine problem, rather than admit he'd simply run out of fuel. Then he explained how his boat had been looted by the pirates and how they had come back with the means to steal his boat. Then he told them about his and Janey's attempts to thwart the pirates and take back his boat, and how he had witnessed a shooting in cold blood.

The two detectives looked at each other. 'Yes, we understand you were shot, Mr Mathews.'

'Yes, I got shot. But I also witnessed the murder of another man.'

One of the detectives got up and went outside the room to use his phone.

It was then explained to Travis that their line of enquiry had changed because of what he had just told them, and that what had started out as charge of piracy, kidnap and attempted murder had now become a murder investigation.

'And what happened to the body of the man you claim was shot and killed?' one of the detectives asked Travis.

Travis closed his eyes and remembered the moment the pirate captain had shot through one of his own crew. He lowered his voice. 'He was shot on my boat. I buried him in a sandy grave on the island.'

Did you mark the grave, Mr Mathews?'

He nodded. 'Yeah, of course. I used some rocks to mark the place.'

The officers said someone from homicide would be in touch with him soon.

Travis looked pained. 'Can't you just give them a copy of the statement I just gave you?'

He leaned back on his pillows and closed his eyes again. Talking about it had brought it all back; the good and bad. His head played a montage of images like a video stream. They were all of Janey.

*Janey as he first saw her, standing on the quayside in her see-through dress.*

*Janey refusing his sandwiches and storming off to lock herself in his cabin.*

*Janey blowing up his radio.*

*Kissing her at the top of the waterfall.*

*Janey giving him the kiss of life and then really kissing him on the edge of the cliff.*

He thought about that kiss for a good long while.


In the suite at their hotel, Janey took a long warm shower and washed her hair. It felt really good to feel clean and smell fresh again. She sat on the sofa to drink another cup of sweet tea to wash down a couple of the painkillers she'd been prescribed. Her head was throbbing.

Mark watched her intently.

'Are you okay?' she asked him, thinking that really it should be him asking her that question.

He shook his head. 'No, I'm not okay, Janey. I thought you were dead. I have suffered so much.'

She looked at him. His eyes were bloodshot and his skin was sallow. He looked completely unravelled, which so wasn't like him. He was usually so capable and unruffled.

She put down her tea and held her arms open to him. 'Oh, Mark, come here, sweetheart. I can only imagine what you've been though. I don't know how I'd have managed if the situation had been in reverse and it had been you missing and presumed dead. Especially while we were on a foreign trip.'

But he didn't come to her; instead he began to pace the room anxiously.

'And you look so different, Janey. To be honest, I hardly recognised you. I don't like that you are so different. In just a week, your skin is darker and your hair is lighter, and your face, well… it's different. It's like it's not you who's come back.'

She watched him with concern as he wrung his hands and walked up and down the same strip of floor over and over.

'But, Mark, I was outside a lot and the sun bleached my hair and made my skin darker. I've lost a bit of weight too, but I'm still me. I'm still the same Janey. I'm still *your* Janey.'

'We need to talk,' he told her. 'We need to talk about you being with that man alone on an island for a week. I want to know every detail, so that we can rationalise what happened and decide how to proceed with our litigation for compensation.'

She sighed. 'Oh, Mark, I got castaway on an island and kidnapped by modern day pirates. Believe me when I tell you, that this was nothing like the *Pirates of the Caribbean* movie. I was very lucky to get out of the whole awful situation alive, so can't we just leave it at that?'

'No, we cannot, because we might have a strong legal case here!'

*He was trying to wrangle a lawsuit out of all of this?*

*He couldn't be serious?*

'What about Travis Mathews? He must be guilty of something. What did he do to you on that island, Janey?'

He was starting to annoy her now. '*Do to me*? Travis Mathews saved my life. You should be thanking him, not trying to sue him!'

Mark gave her an angry sideways glance. 'I'm sure you thanked him enough for both of us.'

She was aghast. '*What?* What do you mean by that, Mark?'

'You heard me. I saw how you were with him at the hospital, fawning over him, spilling tears. There is a name for it, you know. It's a recognised condition. It's called Stockholm Syndrome. I've come across it several times. It happens to a victim when she bonds with her captor.'

'*Captor?* What *are* you talking about? I wasn't captured by Travis!'

Janey picked up her tea again. She sipped it slowly. Stress, she had to remember, affected people in different ways, and Mark had clearly been deeply affected by her being missing.

'So you think that something happened on that island between me and Travis?'

'Well, did it?'

Janey furrowed her brow. The movement tugged at the sutures in her forehead. She considered the question for a moment and decided to be honest about it. She opened her mouth to admit that yes, something had happened on that island, except that Mark didn't give her the chance.

'Because we searched for days and every day that went by, it became more and more likely that you weren't coming back. I thought you were dead. I was *told* you were dead. Honey said she was lonely and afraid, and I felt lonely and afraid too. You see, we were both grieving, and we only had each other. We spent a lot of time in each other's company, both day and night, just like you and Travis did on that island.'

Janey's mouth had dropped open at hearing this almost manic tirade.

'Are you trying to tell me something about you and Honey?'

Mark lowered his head and closed his eyes.

Her tea cup flipped over and the contents were spilled. 'Mark... are you and Honey... in love with her or something?'

'Good grief, no!' he insisted. 'I don't love her. I still love you.'

Janey mopped up the mess, thinking the hotel would no doubt bill them for the fluffy white gown now it was ruined. 'Well, thank goodness, Mark. You had me worried there for a minute.'

'And that's what makes it so difficult to explain to you. You see, it was only sex, and I can assure you that it meant nothing to me, Janey. You could say that I was simply a victim of circumstance in a highly stressful situation.'

Janey stared at him in disbelief; she had an awful image in her head of him and the voluptuous Honey in bed together. She thought she might be sick. Mark was still talking to her as if presenting a well-rehearsed defence case in court.

'Mark...!' she interrupted. 'I think you're right. It was a highly stressful time. I'm sure there's a name for it, a recognised condition, for having sex with someone else while your fiancée is missing and presumed dead.'

He looked relieved. 'Yes, there probably is. I'm sure you're right, Janey.'

'That name is *cheating bastard*, Mark. And it happens when someone can't be trusted!'

He began pleading. 'But, Janey, darling, I can assure you it will never ever happen again.'

'Really? Is that so? Because in my experience of your OCD, you'll want to cheat on me at least once a week for the rest of my life!'

She then told him that she had a splitting headache and needed to rest.

'And, Mark... I suggest you find yourself another room.'


Later that evening, she took a taxi to the hospital and was surprised to see the media camped out in force. Unbeknown to her, there had been a lot of news interest in the search for her and Travis and, more recently, in the capture of the pirates who had kidnapped and attacked them.

Janey was quickly recognised from the picture that her family had released.

'How are you feeling now, Ms Sinclair, after your terrible ordeal?'

'Do you know if Mr Mathews will ever fully recover from his shooting?'

Luckily, the hospital staff spotted her too and whisked her quickly through the doors and into the side ward, where she could be reunited with Travis. She was dizzy with excitement at the thought of seeing him again and had to steady herself. She had wondered, on her way over there, what she would do if Honey was at his bedside, as she wasn't quite sure how she would handle seeing her so soon after Mark's shocking confession. Fortunately, when she was escorted to Travis's room she found he was all alone, sitting propped up against a pile of white pillows. He had a clean dressing wrapped around his shoulder.

'Hi there, Captain Mathews,' she said cheerfully from the doorway.

He waved his good arm. His face was pale and still unshaven. 'Hi, Janey. I was just sitting here hoping you'd come and say goodbye to me before you flew back to Scotland.'

'What?' She was a little taken aback. 'You thought I might not come? Travis, I needed to know that you're okay. I mean, you almost died.'

He shook his head. 'That's just ridiculous. I didn't almost die.'

Suddenly, she noticed he wasn't looking at her and had a real sense that something had changed between them. Where was her confident and friendly captain?

*Where was the brave and clever man she'd known on the island?*

*Where did her fellow adventurer go?*

*Where was the man who'd kissed her so passionately?*

It was as if, now that they were back in the real world, he'd put up a wall to keep her out. Her heart suddenly became unreasonably heavy and began to thump hard against her ribs.

'Have you seen your family yet?' she asked him, trying to keep the conversation light.

'Yeah, they just left. My ex-wife too. For a moment there, when I opened my eyes, I thought I'd died and gone to hell.'

They laughed together but it sounded stilted.

Then there was a long and deafening silence.

Janey thought again about Honey and Mark but she thought it best not to say anything.

*This was so awkward.*

*This was excruciatingly painful.*

He indicated to the sutures on her forehead. 'And how are you feeling?'

She shrugged. 'Oh yeah, I'm just fine.'

*Did they really have to do this small talk?*

*Why didn't they just say what needed to be said to each other? They'd had a larger than life experience together, surely that couldn't be ignored?*

He was now staring out of the window. His jaw was gritted. A pulse throbbing in his cheek.

*Was he in pain, or just struggling with what to say to her next?*

*This was horribly uncomfortable.*

*Why wouldn't he even look at her?*

Tears swelled up in her eyes, threatening to spill down her cheeks, and a lump of grief formed in her throat. Embarrassed, she turned to walk away.

'Well, good luck, then. I'll be going.' she managed to say. But then, finding it impossible to leave things that way between them, she turned on her heels and said to him in a voice that sounded almost like she was begging, 'Travis, please tell me. Did something naturally happen between us on that island or did I just imagine it?'

He nodded and a slow smile spread across his mouth, making his bottom lip quiver.

'Yeah, I think we had something going there for a while, didn't we?'

She hesitated at the door, filled with anticipation over what he might say next.

'But like you once said to me, Janey. It's best we don't start what we can't naturally finish.'

His words cut through her heart like a knife.

*He was saying no. He was saying goodbye.*

Humiliated, she walked out the door and didn't look back.

In boarding her British Airways flight back to the UK, Janey's heart sank to unimaginable levels when she realised she was going to be seated mid-plane on a row of four seats in economy class, with Mark on one side of her and her parents on the other. The one and only available premium seat had, to Mark's annoyance, been offered to Gwen at the check-in and she had accepted it.

As they tried to settle into their cramped seats, Mark did nothing but hiss and complain.

She heard him saying to the man sitting next to him on the other side of the narrow isle, how he was used to turning left into first class and not being herded into economy, with 'all the rabble'.

She didn't know if she or the man subjected to this statement had been more mortified.

In contrast, her parents were sitting in stony-faced silence, because they'd noticed that she and Mark had hardly been speaking to each other. Her mother kept whispering little disparaging quips, and her father kept shaking his head and rubbing his prominent forehead with one hand, as if he was in dismay and not delight that his daughter had been found alive and well.

Janey was resolved to let them think whatever they wanted, and reminded herself that if she could survive being castaway on an island and being kidnapped by pirates, then she should be able to deal with ten hours in a confined space with the three people she least wanted to be with right now.

But it was a tough call.

After listening to Mark continuing to bicker about economy in-flight services, she suggested to him that he take some of his anxiety pills and get some sleep. Then she remembered how she had spat the last she had of them out of her mouth into the sand on the island. Her mind was playing tricks with her because everything she said or did triggered flashbacks.

She'd been warned that this would happen, that it was part of her trauma recovery. Even so, her heart pitched painfully in her chest at the memory. It had been just before Travis had untied her from the tree and rescued her from the pirates, when she had been angry with him for not heading back to Antigua to get help. When he had told her that she already had help – she had him – and that there was no way he would leave her behind on that island.

She closed her eyes to stem the tears and tried to feign sleep.

# Chapter Twelve

Despite being wrapped up in her winter coat, Janey Sinclair was shivering as she marched over North Bridge in the direction of her office. It was almost the middle of March and Edinburgh was still freezing. She sighed as she pushed her way through the heavy swing doors of the old building that housed her offices. Her steps echoed on the polished cold marble floor of the foyer as she followed the white lines of icy light that streamed in from tall glass windows. She took the lift to the top floor and stepped out into the bustling reception area of *Hot Scot Magazine*.

'Janey, you are just in time to help me choose our July cover!' enthused Gwen, who held up two contenders. 'A highland landscape or a silhouetted castle ruin?'

'I think the castle ruin would be perfect,' Janey suggested, while quickly removing her coat and scarf. At her desk, Janey began to reply to her emails and check her schedule: advertising meeting, budget meeting, editorial meeting.

'Oh, please save me from meetings,' she muttered to no one but herself.

Then something caught her eye on the BBC World News in the corner of her computer screen and she immediately clicked to enlarge it. Her stomach flipped over as she recognised the five men pictured. It was an international news story about the pirates who had kept her captive on the island and who had looted Travis's boat and shot him.

'Pirates captured off the Virgin Islands in the Caribbean Sea have been charged with numerous offenses including murder, attempted murder, kidnap and tyranny, and are now being held in custody while awaiting trial, set for the end of the month. Bail has been refused,' the news anchorman read out.

Janey was in a cold sweat. This news wasn't going to help with her nightmares and reoccurring flashbacks, but she did feel proud of herself for having something to do with their capture. In fact, she'd have loved to see the look on their faces when the coastguard had turned up to arrest them while they'd had no means of escape.

She knew from speaking with the police detectives before she left Antigua that Travis had given a full statement and agreed to testify in court. This was because he had witnessed a murder and he had been the only eye witness. She had been told, after giving her statement, that she could press criminal charges against the pirates and sue for damages if she wished to do so. Mark had told her that she should, but she had decided against it for personal reasons, as she had been more than keen to leave the island after her final conversation with Travis, and didn't ever plan to return.

On the newsreel, to the jeers of an angry crowd outside the court, the pirates were being escorted to prison vans. She watched the spectacle and winced as the men struggled against their captures. The big scary pirate captain, the accused killer, hissed and spat at the crowd.

Her phone rang. It was her assistant. 'Janey, there is a delivery for you.'

'Okay, thanks. Send it in.'

She was expecting her layout proofs, but instead it was an enormous bouquet of flowers blocking the doorway of her office space. She frowned; no doubt another pathetic attempt by Mark to get her to change her mind and marry him. He had been sending flowers, letters and gifts to her office daily now for almost a week. Yesterday had been a poetry-o-gram, for goodness' sake.

She'd officially broken off their engagement yet he had refused to accept it.

'Erm, where do you want them, madam?' The delivery man was wobbling under the weight of the flora and foliage, while glancing at her coffee table and suggesting it to her with his eyes.

She marched over to the bouquet to pluck out the card.

*Darling Janey, forgive me. I would never have had sex with another woman if I hadn't thought you were already dead.*

'Charming. Return to sender, please.'


Travis took *The Mermaid* out of the marina well before dawn in a stealth-like way. He'd been carefully planning this covert mission while in his sick bed, recovering from a couple of complications that had extended his hospital stay to a full week. Somehow, he'd managed to catch a secondary infection and, ridiculously, they wouldn't let him out until he'd finished a course of antibiotics. He'd wanted to discharge himself, except that an administrator had warned his health insurance wouldn't pay out unless a doctor officially signed him out and, as his medical bill amounted to many thousands of dollars, he'd had to remain their reluctant prisoner.

But now he was free at last and he was back on his boat.

The homicide detectives had advised him to lie low until the trial, so as far as anyone was concerned, this little jaunt could be counted as doing exactly that, and besides, no one would guess that he'd want to go straight back to the place he'd had so much trouble escaping from just a week earlier.

Once he was out into the open water, he thought once again about Janey: beautiful, clever, brave Janey. The look of hurt on her face as he denied having any interest in her had almost killed him then and it was still haunting him now.

He had desperately wanted to get out of that hospital bed and go after her, but instead he'd had to close his eyes and listen to the sound of her footsteps walking away. He'd never felt so bad in his life, and that was saying something. But to have done otherwise would have put her life in danger.

His heart felt heavy as he sighed and inhaled warm salty air into his lungs.

Just hours after giving his statement to the homicide detectives, he'd received death and blackmail threats from associate pirates and felons, telling him not to testify in the murder trail.

Janey's name had been mentioned in those threats.

He'd reported this, of course, and he'd been offered police protection, but when it came to Janey's safety, the detective's words *'Our best advice would be that she leave the Caribbean as soon as possible'* still rang in his head.

He knew he'd done the right thing in sending her away. It was the only thing he could do to protect her, but based on what she'd said to him at the hospital, he'd more than once considered caving in and not testifying, but what would that achieve except to put a killer pirate back on the water and make the world no safer for anyone – including him and Janey.

So now he was torturing himself with the daydream that she actually might have stayed.


Back in Edinburgh, after what had been yet another gruelling day at the office, Janey went home to her small apartment to sit on her sofa and eat pizza. She flicked through the menu of adventure movies and tried to watch one but couldn't concentrate. She felt so horribly alone. She still had her network of girlfriends and they'd each called after hearing about her ordeal, encouraging her to go out on the town with them for drinks and to the cinema, but she'd insisted that she had to get over her jet lag first. Which was, of course, just an excuse because what she wanted to do was wallow for a while in the hope that she could make sense of all that had happened over the past couple of weeks. Real life, as she called it, back here in Scotland, didn't seem enough for her any more.

She lay on her sofa, going over and over every single detail of her time on the island with Travis.

She revisited every conversation she ever had with him. She certainly couldn't stop thinking of him, fantasising about him and what he might be doing right at that moment. She was drawn to sad songs that reflected the way she felt and she ended up in tears over and over again, mourning what had been and what would never be. She feared that she had fallen in love with him.

It certainly felt that way and it hurt.

Travis, she decided, was guarding his heart. It was the only explanation for his behaviour. He'd been married once and he'd been hurt in the cruellest way possible, so she could understand that, when faced with new feelings, he'd put up barriers.

Well, now her heart was broken too, so should she do the same? Guard it? Let no one touch it? Then at some point in the future, when she had some distance between now and then, she would know neither love nor pain? Travis had called it 'keeping things simple'.

From her slumped position in the sitting room, she could see into her bedroom, where her suitcase was sitting. It was exactly where she'd left it, unopened, and so it had become her Pandora's Box. If she opened it, then amongst her unworn holiday clothes and hardly used sun lotions, she would see all the evidence of her recent trauma.

Perhaps even a few grains of sand from a Caribbean beach?

She took a deep breath and got to her feet. The sooner she got everything unpacked and put away at the very back of her wardrobe, then the sooner she could move on and forget that she'd ever been to Antigua or met Captain Travis Mathews.

She clicked open the locks and unzipped the case. Immediately, the scent of the Caribbean rose from her belongings and filled her senses, her version of the Caribbean at least. How amazing that even a hint of certain smells and sounds, like perfumes or a song, had the power to take a person back to a certain time and place.

She remembered the coin that Travis had given her in the cave and all the questions that the pirate had about it. For some reason, she'd instinctively lied about where it had been found, and she started to wonder why she'd done that?

Then she thought about the story that Travis had told her about a missing boat full of silver coins and, suddenly, she'd forgotten all about unpacking, because something in the subconscious part of her brain had clicked into overdrive.

She switched on her laptop and did a search for any information she might find on pirate treasure and shipwrecks in the Caribbean and specifically the date 1732.

After a few minutes of searching, her eyes widened when she saw a picture of the exact coin that Travis had placed in her hand. It was for sale on a collectable and rare coin website.

*A very rare Spanish Eight Reales, Pillar Dollar, dated 1732 in extra fine condition and over ninety percent silver composition. Due to its rarity: price only upon application. Historical documents show that this coin is from one of two large cargos of newly minted silver Pillar Dollars seized by mutinying pirates in the Caribbean Sea. One boat was successfully found and confiscated by The Governor of the British Virgin Islands of that time and its consignment returned to Spain, but the other is still listed as missing to this day, having never been found.*

She re-read the words *rare* and *listed as missing* over again.

Her eyes narrowed as she slowly came to realise what Travis was likely to be up to, and what the pirates had been looking for all along – the lost treasure!

What if Travis had given her the coin as a souvenir simply to play down its importance and throw her off thinking that it had any meaning?

He seemed to know the story of the missing boat full of silver coins very well indeed.

Had he realised immediately what he'd found in that cave?

Suddenly Janey was sitting up poker straight in her chair. He must have known from the moment he clocked eyes on the date 1732 that, if the haul of lost silver from the second boat had been hidden in that cave, then there would be untold riches to claim. How dare he give her the cold shoulder like that, breaking her heart, knowing full well that she'd go running straight back to the UK, just so he could then go back to *their* cave to find *their* treasure and keep it all for himself!

Janey wasted no time in phoning her boss to ask for some more time off. She didn't offer any real explanation, except to say that she had to 'straighten a few things out' before she could come back to work.

Gwen, who was receiving therapy to help her manage the guilt she still felt about sending Janey on her castaway and kidnapping ordeal, didn't ask for one. She simply told her to 'take all the time she needed'.

So Janey locked her suitcase and went back online to book the next available seat on a flight out to Antigua. She was up for a new Caribbean adventure, and this time she was ready and willing to tackle anything. There was no way that Travis was doing this without her.

# Chapter Thirteen

Travis had a new plan and he'd thought of nothing else for the past week. He'd convinced himself that he knew where the missing hoard of 1732 silver coins had been hidden for all these years. He'd decided that it wasn't in the cave where he'd found the coin. In fact, the more he'd thought about it, the less likely it could be the right place.

For one thing, the layout of the cave was shallow and didn't lend itself as a good hiding place. It was also home to an established colony of bats, evident in the floor being deep in bat guano, which would certainly have been several metres lower in 1732 than it was today. Which begged the question as to how this single silver coin was lying so close to the surface. It had to have been dropped there far more recently.

So he'd made several assumptions: he guessed that the pirates, who had been operating notoriously in the BVIs for many years plundering boats and stealing stuff, had been searching for these particular silver coins for a while and that they had indeed already found them. His second assumption was that they'd had a twice-thieving-mutineer in their midst (them already being thieves), which would further explain why the coin was in the other cave, and why the pirates were so jumpy, unpredictable, and willing to kill each other and anyone else who got between them and their treasure.

But then he wondered why, when they knew these islands better than anyone, they had they made that particular island, and that particular cave, their secret HQ.

Did they have some sort of intelligence (although he used the term advisedly where these idiots were concerned) like maybe from an old map or something that had led them to this particular place? They had certainly been overly suspicious, aggressive, and possessive about why he and Janey were on the island, and they'd asked them questions about the coin and where he'd found it.

The only thing he couldn't get his head around was why, if they were in fact sitting on millions of dollars worth of silver coins would they a) keep it hidden and not sell it, and b) still feel the need to plunder boats, kidnap people, and rob stuff.

He had deduced that the coins had to be somewhere on the island and most likely in their hideaway cave. His mood lightened as he visualised himself finding the treasure and, if the coin he'd already found was any indication, he guessed it must all be in a place suited to preserving a mint-like condition. He imagined shining his torch on it all for it to shine back at him in a shimmering radiance. He'd be rich beyond his wildest dreams and, once all the drama of the court case against the pirates was over and they were all doing maximum time, he could sell it all off to the highest bidders and start afresh by opening up his own restaurant at last.

Opening a seafood restaurant was something he'd come here to do after his divorce and yet, due to a lack of funding and the recession, he'd not yet managed it. He imagined himself sending an invitation to the grand opening of his restaurant to Janey, at her offices at *Hot Scot* in Edinburgh. He'd include a first class airline seat, and she'd come flying back to him and be so delighted and impressed with his restaurant, and with the fabulous lobster dish he would cook for her, that she'd be swept right off her feet and into his arms.

The other guy, her Mr Fancy-Pants fiancé, could take a hike, as far as he was concerned.

He found himself laughing heartily at his imaginings as he steered *The Mermaid* into the night, back to the island he'd been so keen to escape from only several days earlier.

Janey's flight touched down at noon, Caribbean time. As she left the airport with her suitcase and bag, she breathed in the hot, heavy humid breeze outside the terminal. She waved one arm in the air to flag down a taxi. 'St John's, please!'

She slid into the air-conditioned vehicle and turned back her watch with great satisfaction. Her journey across the Atlantic might have taken almost ten hours but she had just miraculously gained six. She searched through her hand luggage for her sunglasses, and wasted no time checking into her hotel, freshening up, and then heading down to the marina.

She walked onto the wharf and went straight to *The Mermaid's* mooring point.

Every step she took along the boardwalk reminded her of the last time she had been here trying to charter a boat, when she'd taken one look at the weather-beaten old *Mermaid* and her intimidating captain, and decided against both. Yet fate had brought them together.

Now, here she was again, only this time on unfinished business. She was determined that Travis Mathews wasn't going treasure hunting without her.

Except that *The Mermaid's* mooring point was empty.

'Can I help you?' said a voice from behind her.

Janey turned to see a tall, thin, older man. He sported a mahogany brown tan with short grey stubble that went all the way around his face and his head. He was wearing a set of oily overalls and looking at her curiously.

'Yes, I was looking for Travis Mathews. Do you know him?'

'Yeah, I'm Bill. I know him like he's my own brother, but if you see him before I do then maybe you can tell him that he owes me fifty bucks for the fuel he took from my shed this morning.'

She held out her hand. 'I'm Janey.'

Bill jabbed a hand into hers and shook it. 'Yeah, I recognise you. You're the girl who got stuck on the island with him?'

She smiled and nodded in the direction of the empty mooring. 'Do you know where he might have gone?'

'No, he's only just got out of hospital and I've been worried about him because of what's just been on the news. He usually tells me where he's headed, but he just took off.'

Janey shrugged. 'If his boat's not here and he actually remembered to take fuel with him this time, he's more likely to have gone fishing rather than missing, don't you think?'

Bill shook his head. 'I'd agree with you except that now the killer pirate has escaped from jail and Travis is the key witness, I fear he could be in some kinda' trouble.'

Janey looked at him in astonishment. 'What? The killer pirate has escaped? When?'

'This morning. It was on the TV news.'

'Bill, do you have a boat?'


Three hours later, as dawn was breaking over the island's two massive peaks, Travis navigated his way along the coastline and past the beach where he and Janey had set up their original camp as castaways. He made his way around the headland and put *The Mermaid* very carefully into a narrow entrance near the blow hole cave. It was low tide, so he dropped anchor, knowing she'd be safe here while he took his time inside the cave. He waded ashore with his sack of equipment: a powerful torch, a shovel, a metal detector and some strong sacks.

He could hardly wait to start searching for the treasure.

He climbed over some large rocks and then made his way to the entrance of the cave. Once inside, he stopped and took a long look around him. The light from the blow hole lit up the circular pool beneath it. The water acted like a mirror, reflecting light into every nook and cranny, and lighting up the waterfall cascading in from a crack high in the rocks.

He set down his equipment and wondered where to look for the coins first. They had to be in here somewhere, he felt sure of it, and they had to be hidden well enough that the customs officials hadn't managed to find them when they came to clear out all the boxes and crates and pallets of stolen stuff that he'd seen in here. That was all gone now, confiscated by the authorities. No doubt he'd have to fill in some long official claim form just to get back his own box of personal stuff.

*The waterfall? Could there perhaps be a secret grotto behind it?*

The possibility was worth checking it out before he started looking elsewhere. As he stripped down to his undershorts he heard a noise behind him. He turned to find that he wasn't here alone and he blinked his eyes in disbelief.

*'What the…? How the…?'*

The killer pirate captain was standing there and he had a gun in his hand. He swung it hard at Travis's head and unbalanced him, knocking him to his knees.

Travis swore loudly and cradled his split head in his hands. 'Fucking hell! That fucking hurt!'

'I have to wonder how many lives you have left, Captain Mathews,' the pirate said calmly, as he cocked the gun and took aim. 'Is this not my third attempt at killing you?'

Travis raised his bloodied hands in surrender and tried to think of a way out of what had suddenly become a very bad situation indeed.

*How the fuck had this man escaped from custody and a top security jail?*

'How about we talk about this, man to man?' Travis begged.

'You came here to take my silver, no?'

'Look, why don't we do a deal?'

'Are you about to tell me that my coins are the price for you not testifying against me?'

'Yes. That's it. I'll retract my statement and you'll walk away a free man.'

'Or, I could just kill you, and you won't need to retract anything,' the pirate growled.

'How about we split the treasure fifty–fifty and we both walk away from this?' Travis suggested.

The pirate laughed. 'You're not walking anywhere, and this time I will make sure you die here and your troublesome body is never found. Your boat will soon be nothing more than ash blowin' in the breeze, and the location of this cave will once again remain a closely guarded secret.'

At the mention of his boat, Travis buckled. 'Okay, I'm gonna die, so tell me something? Tell me why you didn't cash it all in and get rich?'

The pirate laughed again and shook his head. 'If only it was that simple.'

'Look, I'll admit, I came here to look for the coins. But I still don't know exactly where you have them hidden. So you and me, we could still do a deal. It's not too late!'

The pirate sighed wearily, as if he might have actually been thinking about it. Then he smiled. 'I have decided that I will allow you the privilege of seeing my treasure before you die, Captain Mathews.'

Travis tried to smile too, while sincerely hoping the privilege also offered him a way to escape.

The pirate threw Travis a hessian sack. Inside it was a diver's face mask and weight belt.

'You will need those. Just don't bother taking the belt off when you get down there.'

Travis eyed the pool. So that's where the coins were, at the bottom of the pool all this time!

He started breathing rapidly, hyperventilating, to take in as much air into his body as he could. Saturating his body with oxygen might give him a couple more minutes underwater before he drowned.

However, it wouldn't stop him bleeding to death from his head wound or from getting shot. He took his time attaching the belt to his waist and the mask to his face. He was breathing furiously now and the pirate might assume it was in panic.

The pirate waved the gun. 'Go. Get into the pool. Enjoy!'

Afraid that there might be bullet coming to help him on his way, Travis did as instructed and duck-dived down into the pool, where the centre was one deep vertical abyss.

He kicked his legs and swam fast. He hardly had time to try to equalise the water pressure on his ears as he dropped head first with the weights on him, like a stone, metre upon metre until he was at what he guessed must be a depth of around eighteen metres.

At the bottom of the watery pit visibility was good, as the light from above continued to filter through. He soon realised that he was looking at a pile of silver coins that lay like shimmering fish scales on the sand just beneath him and, for a moment, he was so excited that he forgot he had no air tank on his back and he let some of his precious air escape from his lungs.

He picked up one of the coins and studied it. It was in absolutely perfect condition, like new, and dated, quite unbelievably, 1732. The connection between time and history lay in his fingers and he felt honoured by it. Although time was relative, or so it seemed, and he knew that he had less than five minutes before he passed out and drowned.

He looked up and saw a dark menacing shadow in the bright circle of light far above him. The pirate was keeping a timely vigil to make sure he drowned for sure this time.

To preserve his air and his sanity, Travis tried to keep his heart rate steady and slow and to remain calm. But soon it became evident that the low oxygen level in his brain was beginning to reach a critical level. He was aware of dizziness and a little disorientation.

Only a moment later, and this all felt like a strange dream. He distracted himself by looking again at the coins. They looked like they belonged on a mermaid's tail. His lungs felt like they were bursting and so he had to let out a few bubbles from his mouth. It was no use now anyway as it was mostly carbon dioxide. Once he started exhaling, however, he found he couldn't stop, and soon his lungs had emptied.

He watched the exodus of bubbles slowly expand as they made their way to the surface and he struggled to hold off what had become the inevitable: the watery gasp, the choking as his throat closed up and he tried to stop the awful act of drowning.

His plan had been to release the weight belt as soon as the pirate had left, but the shadow of the pirate was still there looking down at him, like a devil waiting for a soul.

He felt his body relax. Another few seconds and he doubted he would have neither the strength nor the inclination to undo the belt buckle. He'd expected his life to flash before him as he faced his death, but it hadn't so far, and so he decided to make a last conscious wish before the water took him. He wasn't a religious man and he didn't have many regrets in life, but if there was by any chance something after death, another life or another place, then he hoped next time around he had another chance with Janey, that he had the chance to be honest with her and tell her that something *had* happened between them on the island. And he'd fallen quite hopelessly in love with her.

## Chapter Fourteen

Bill's boat, the *Salva Vida*, was a plush, modern and streamlined vessel. It had a light fibreglass hull and two powerful engines, so Janey felt confident they would get to the island in good time.

'What makes you think that Travis would have headed back to the island?' Bill asked her.

'Oh, he left something there and he said he'd be going back for it later.'

Once they reached the familiar shaped island, Janey considered it with mixed feelings. Her life had been turned upside down thanks to this place, and she didn't know whether to feel good about that or not. She tried to recall the exact location of the cave that they had been in and where Travis had found the coin. The coastline in front of them was both jagged and undulating. There were plenty of pretty half moon shaped coves with white sand beaches, and there were dozens of inlets and ingresses that the weather had carved from the rocks and where the sea had now invaded.

It all looked very different from offshore.

After a while, Bill suggested that they just look out for *The Mermaid* instead.

So they made their way around the headland while Janey looked through a pair of binoculars.

She shouted out when she recognised the beach where she and Travis had set up camp, and then she followed her line of sight to the headland, to the place she knew they would find 'their' cave.

'There…' she said, pointing a finger. 'That's it! That's the cave where he found it.'

Bill looked at her curiously. 'Found what?'

Janey immediately shut her big mouth. *Had she just said that aloud?*

'Call me suspicious, but I think there's something you're not telling *me,* young lady. Found what?'

'Erm, a coin… a silver reale. It's what the old pirates used to call a piece of eight.'

Bill's eyes narrowed. 'I do happen to know what a silver reale is. Why do you think they call me Booty Bill?'

She wondered for a moment why that name sounded strangely familiar to her? 'Erm, 'cos you like to wear boots?'

Booty pointed to the flip-flops on his feet. 'You think?'

Suddenly, out of the corner of her eye she saw a boat. 'There!' she shouted. 'In that narrow cove. I can just see her.' She handed the binoculars to Bill.

He took them and focussed them on the partially visible boat and shook his head. 'No, that's not *The Mermaid.*'

'Really?' Janey bit her lip anxiously.

Bill steered the *Salva Vida* into the next cove; the advantage of having a shallow hull was that they could almost get into the beach.

'I'll go ashore and see what's going on,' he said. 'Give me just one hour and then, if I'm not back, you must call the coastguard for back up. Right?'

Janey was not impressed with this plan. 'Look, Bill, if that is the killer pirate's boat over there and he tries to use it to escape, someone has to man the radio and go chasing after him at high speed. That someone should be you!'

Bill was still thinking about this while Janey prepared to leave the boat. 'If I'm wrong, and it's just a nice family having a picnic on the beach, then I'll be straight back.'

She took the binoculars, a torch and a flare gun, and stuffed them all into a bag that she wrapped securely around her body.

'Here, wait,' said Bill 'I really think you might need this…'

She turned round to see him pointing a gun at her.

'Bloody hell, Bill. Put that away. I don't even know how to fire a gun and I certainly don't think I could ever shoot anyone!'

Reluctantly, he put the gun back in the wheelhouse. 'Remember that the tide's turning,' he warned.

Janey nodded. 'Okay. Give me an hour but in all likelihood, I'll be back well before then.'

Bill fiddled with his watch and gave her the 'okay' sign with his thumb and forefinger.

Janey waded ashore in water that was thigh deep. She could see that the tide was coming in fast. She reached the beach and ran along it, then she climbed up to the top of the headland where she would be afforded a good view of the unidentified boat. Once there, she lay flat on her tummy, to stay out of sight and also to get her breath back. She saw two boats in the narrow ingress.

*The Mermaid* was bobbing about in front of the other boat, which had blocked its exit.

That itself looked menacing.

She studied the lie of the land. This was the proximity of the blow hole cave but as far as she knew, the entrance to this cave was on the other side of the cove, although from here it looked like there might be another way in. She took out the binoculars.

Yes, there was a deep crease in the rock that might be worth investigating. If it was an alternative route into the cave system, it would mean she didn't have to climb up another rock face and onto another headland. She zoomed in with the binoculars and focussed on the potential entrance in time to see a dark shape emerging from it. She jumped back in fear.

It was the killer pirate captain!

He came out from the darkness into the bright sunlight, stopped and shaded his eyes as he quickly looked around.

Janey ducked down to keep out of his line of sight and then she watched as he made his way back to his boat. She held her breath as he boarded his vessel.

To her horror, she then saw him pick up what looked to be a fuel can and take it over to *The Mermaid*. He sprinkled liquid over the deck and inside the wheelhouse while she could do nothing but to watch, helpless, as he struck a match and Travis's boat began to burn.

The killer pirate then hurried back to his boat and manoeuvred it carefully out of the channel.

Only when he had begun his getaway, could she risk sliding down the rock and shingle slope to the base of the cove, yelling out Travis's name.

*God forbid he was on board The Mermaid?*

The boat was now too engulfed in flames to go aboard and check. She gulped back her fears, and hoped that her instincts were right and that Travis was in the cave.

*But was he hurt? Was she too late? Was he already dead?*

Her heart was pounding and she was afraid of what she'd find inside, but she rushed into the crease. She made her way inside quickly and through a series of dark damp tunnels. In her rush, she dropped her torch. It bounced and rolled across the floor away from her, clattering across the stone floor, casting a kaleidoscope of light across the walls of the cave.

Janey scrabbled to pick it up and ran on to suddenly emerge in the now familiar big, wide open cavern of the blow hole cave. She stood in the centre of the space, pivoting around slowly on her bare feet and with her eyes searching for Travis. He was nowhere to be seen, and the tide was already coming in.

She glanced over the pool and around the walls, over the ledges and in the clear torrent of the waterfall, and then back again to the pool.

Suddenly there he was, floating face down in the water.

*Oh no, not again. How long had he been there?*

*Was he dead? He certainly looked dead.*

She waded in and dragged him to the edge of the pool while feeling for a pulse. There wasn't one. She rolled him onto his back and saw that his pallor was deathly white. His body felt cold and unresponsive. He wasn't breathing.

*Was he just pretending, like last time, just to get her to kiss him again?*

'Travis, wake up! Stop it. This isn't funny!' she cried, shaking him.

His mouth fell open. His lips were tinged blue.

She floated him to the shallow edge of the pool, hauling out his full wet weight to drier ground.

'Oh, Travis. Please come back,' she begged.

Kneeling over him, she pressed her lips to his to form a seal and forced her air into his lungs. She worked on his heart by pumping her hands against his bare chest. She counted the chest compressions aloud until she was exhausted and weeping, but there was still no response from him; he just lay there, still, and wet and cold.

With tears streamed down her face, she fell onto him, sobbing. She'd lost him.

Then suddenly, he began to move, not slowly, but in violent fit-like jerks.

Janey leapt away to give him some space. 'Travis?'

He was kicking his legs for all he was worth, as if he were still swimming. Then he arched his back and gave out an almighty roar as his lungs sucked in a great volume of air.

This, she decided joyfully, is what must be meant by 'alive and kicking'.

When he was calmer, he rolled onto his side and he started throwing up all the water he had swallowed. She let him recover himself for a moment, while she picked up the silver coin that had just fallen out of his shorts pocket.

'Janey? Are you real or am I imagining you?' he eventually spluttered.

'I'm real. Come on, we've got to get out of here before the whole place floods.'

They staggered through the rising water and Janey pushed him into the passageway that led to the exit. A rush of water accompanied them as they made their escape. Outside, she led him over to a dry spot of ground where he could rest, which he did until he saw the red orange flames and black smoke billowing from his boat in the cove.

Clearly distressed and disorientated, he staggered to his feet only to fall back again and to sit groaning and holding his bleeding head in his hands as he muttered.

*'My Mermaid...'*


Janey could see that Bill was on board *The Mermaid*. He was bravely running around the flaming deck with a foaming fire extinguisher in his hands, and soon *The Mermaid* looked like she had just been through a steamy-hot soapy wash. He waved the all clear once he had managed to check that the fire was under control, and then between them, one on either side of Travis, they managed to get him back to the *Salva Vida*.

Travis swore like a veritable sailor the whole time, totally distraught about his burnt-out boat.

Bill assured him they would return and tow *The Mermaid* back to the marina for repairs.

'She's badly damaged, just like you, my old mate, but I reckon you'll both survive yet.'

While Bill got on the radio to the coastguard with a description of the fugitive pirate's vessel and the approximate coordinates of his heading, Janey grabbed the first aid kit and applied a sterile pad to Travis's head wound. It clearly needed sutures.

'It seems that I can't leave you alone for a minute without you getting into some kind of trouble,' she told him. He was drifting in and out of consciousness. When awake, he made a big fuss about them leaving the island. He yelled about waiting for the tide to turn and going straight back into the cave. He mumbled incoherently about treasure and pirates and pieces of eight.

At least, for Bill's ears, Janey hope it was incoherent.

With Travis resting at the back of the boat, they headed back to Antigua at full speed.

Bill asked Janey what Travis had meant by all his ramblings.

'I think maybe you had better ask Travis that question,' she replied, a little gingerly.

Clearly Booty Bill wasn't stupid. He had already guessed Travis was up to something.

At the hospital, where Travis had become something of a regular celebrity, he was advised to spend the night. He complained bitterly about this and even tried to check himself out, but Janey and Bill managed to persuade him that getting his head wound properly treated and letting the doctors observe him for his suspected concussion should be the only thing on his agenda.

'Everything else,' Janey told him, 'could wait until the next day.'

Bill spoke to the police, and they immediately posted a guard on Travis's room again.

Janey gave her contact details to the nurse on duty. 'This is where I'm staying in town, so if he tries to leave before he is supposed to, or if he causes you any trouble at all, call me straight away.'

Then she went back to her hotel room, took a shower, helped herself to what she considered to be a well-deserved drink from the mini bar, and then drew the blinds, turned up the air-con, and slept like she hadn't slept in years.

In fact, she slept so deeply that she dreamed dark and disturbing dreams all night long.

She dreamt she was on board *The Mermaid* with Travis and they were being chased by pirates. The pirate ship was big and black and menacing. It had the Jolly Roger flying from its mast and its sails were ripped and billowed in the wind as it gained speed on them. Strangely, as it came along side and the pirate crew prepared to board and take them captive, she saw Mark was one of them. He was dressed like Johnny Depp's character, Jack Sparrow, in *Pirates of the Caribbean*. He was laughing at her manically as she woke up in a cold sweat.

The phone in her room was ringing.

'Hello?' she answered it, while checking her watch.

It was eight am.

'Miss Sinclair, there is a gentleman waiting for you in reception.'

'Oh, okay, thank you. Tell him I'll be right down.'

Janey didn't need to ask who the gentleman might be. She dressed quickly in a light blue sleeveless blouse and white tailored shorts. She slid her feet into a pair of gilt espadrilles and made her way down to reception. Travis, she could see, was sitting on a sofa, reading a boating magazine. He wore a Panama hat, tilted jauntily to one side of his head, no doubt to hide his latest hospital dressing.

'Hey, Travis, you want some breakfast?' she said, approaching him.

He put the magazine down and rose to his feet. 'Yeah, thanks. I'm starved. They don't feed you properly in hospital.'

She linked her arm through his and they made their way through the foyer to an air-conditioned garden room. The furniture was colonial and there were lots of palm style plants in big pots positioned between the tables to afford guests their privacy. They chose a table for two by the window and sat opposite each other. Travis politely removed his hat. Janey had to stop herself from visibly wincing at the large square gauze dressing that covered his sutures.

A waiter attended to them. Janey ordered tea and Travis ordered coffee.

Then they both silently perused the breakfast menu. The atmosphere between them was excruciatingly weighted with unspoken words.

'I'm not sure what to order. It all looks delicious,' Travis commented, casually.

The waiter approached with their drinks.

'Well, I'd recommend the Captain's Special,' Janey quipped.

'That sounds good to me. What are you having, sweetheart?'

The way he said 'sweetheart' completely threw her. She stared at him with her mouth opening and closing like a fish out of water.

The waiter looked at her encouragingly, his pencil posed. 'Madam?'

'Erm… eggs, scrambled please and a piece of toast. Thank you.'

They resumed their contemplation until Travis's hand reached over the table and gently took hers. She waited for a moment, composing herself, before looking into his eyes and waiting for what he might say to her. Was he going to thank her for saving his life first or tell her how happy he was to see her again?

'Janey, you really shouldn't have come back.'

His gratitude was compelling.

'Despite what you might think, Travis, I didn't just happen to come back here on vacation. On the contrary, I've just about had as much vacation as I'll ever need in my lifetime. No, I came back because it seems you and I have some unfinished business. You see, once I had time to think about things, I realised *exactly* what you are up to and I want you to know that I won't be duped out of my share of the treasure!'

He continued to sip his coffee and, dare she say it, even look amused. 'If I remember correctly, and I think I do… *I* found that coin, not you.'

She picked up her handbag from the floor. She wanted to hit him with it. Instead, she slid her hand into it and placed something down in front of him. It was a coin, which she flipped over so that it was date side up.

She watched the smile drop off his face.

'Well, I found another one. So that makes us equal partners, does it not?' She decided not to mention that it had dropped out of his shorts in the cave yesterday.

He looked at it and gave a low whistle. 'That's my girl!'

'So, let's get one thing straight, Captain Mathews. I'm not *your* girl and neither am I your sweetheart. I'm here on business. Unfinished business. Pure and *simple*. I hope that's clear?' She put the high emphasis on the word 'simple' entirely for his benefit.

He looked pained. 'And how did you know where to find me?'

'The coins, of course. I assumed you'd go straight back to the island.'

'Janey, can I ask you a personal question?'

She rolled her eyes. 'No, you can't. All questions from here on in are to be non-personal.'

'How long do you plan to stay?'

She looked agitated. 'As long as it takes. Why?'

'I ask because if you plan to stay for more than a few days, this hotel will cost you a small fortune, and you might want to consider staying at my place?'

She lifted her chin. 'You're offering me a room at your beach house? Would that be for a fee or for free?'

'Free, of course. It's not too far away from the marina, and you are more than welcome. It's not much, in fact, to be honest...'

'How many bedrooms do you have?'

'One.'

'Then no, thank you. I'll stay here at the hotel. I can easily afford it.'

She wasn't being exactly truthful. The room rate was extortionate and it was all going on her credit card, but she was damned if she was going to keep his bed warm on the nights that Honey wasn't in it.

He looked at her ruefully. 'Actually, I do use one room as a study and so it could easily be a second bedroom.'

'And what about your girlfriend, won't she mind?' she asked him pointedly.

He laughed. 'I thought that all questions were to be non-personal from now on?'

This had almost become some kind of game.

'Actually, Honey went off to work in Florida, so I don't expect I'll see her again.'

Janey quietly finished her tea and tried not to look pleased. When she spoke again it was in relation to his friend Booty Bill.

'Bill asked me yesterday what you were doing on the island.'

'And what did you tell him?'

'Nothing. But I think we should tell him about the treasure and cut him in.'

'Look, Janey. Boots and I go way back but, if it's all the same to you, I'd rather keep him out of this just now.'

'Why? He said he thinks of you as his own brother and besides, he has a boat and we don't.'

Travis laughed again. 'He actually said that? Really? His own brother? Well, the old sea-dog!'

After breakfast was over, they agreed that they should at least go and talk with Bill.

# Chapter Fifteen

They made their way down to the marina, where Bill was aboard the *Salva Vida*.

'Permission to come aboard, captain?' Travis asked him, as they stood by the gang plank.

'Absolutely, come on over. I'm just listenin' on the radio for any news of the killer pirate.'

'Has he been recaptured yet?' Janey asked, as she trundled onto Bill's boat.

'No. He's still out there. He's a sea snake, that one. If he can escape from a high security jail and hide from the coastguard, then no one around here can sleep easy in their bunks until he's found and put back behind bars.'

Travis was momentarily distracted from the conversation by the stark image of his scorched black boat in the next mooring station. Bill noted this and shook his head in despair and sympathy.

'The wheelhouse is totally destroyed, but don't you worry too much, because it can be fixed. I'll help you get her all sorted. It can be a project we can work on together over the next few months.'

'I owe you big time, man. Thanks so much for fetching her home for me.'

'Are you insured by any chance?' Janey asked, looking sadly over at the shadow of *The Mermaid*. She knew nothing about boats but it was obviously going to cost a fortune to fix her up.

'No, I'm afraid not. The choice was between her and me and I won. But that's okay, because I'm hoping to have the means to pay for the repairs very soon.' He turned to Bill. 'And that's what Janey and I wanna' talk to you about this morning, Boots.'

He looked at them curiously and lit a cigarette. 'Okay. I'm all ears.'

Travis looked about them. The marina was busy with people and boats. 'Can we go somewhere a bit quieter, where we won't be overheard?'

Bill fired up the *Salva Vida's* powerful engines and they made their way out to sea.

After a short while, Bill dropped anchor, and he then cracked open a few beers. They sat on deck, on various upturned buckets, facing each other and ready to talk business while the boat rocked gently from side to side.

Travis began to explain. 'When Janey and I were on the island, we came across a cave. I found a coin in there. The date on it made me think on that old legend you told me once, about those two boats full of pirate silver heading for Tortola. You know the one I mean, Boots?'

'Aye, I know the story of the silver coins very well. Everyone around here does. One boat was confiscated when it arrived at Tortola and there's one boat still missing to this very day.'

Travis tossed him the piece of eight that Janey had presented him with that morning.

It spun into the air, catching the sunlight, until Bill caught it. When he opened his hand and saw the date, his eyes opened so wide that it looked like his eyeballs might pop out of his head and roll across the deck.

'And that's what I was doing in that cave yesterday – trying to find out where the pirates had hidden the lost coins,' Travis continued.

'How did you even suspect they had them?' Bill asked, in continued astonishment.

'I had a hunch. Once I saw the date on that first coin, my mind starting working overtime.'

'Me too,' Janey added. 'I suspected that Travis might be up to something, so I came back. The only thing I can't fathom is, if the pirates had already found the coins, why they hadn't sold them all on by now and become rich. It doesn't make sense.' Janey shrugged.

Travis piped up that he'd been trying to fathom that one too.

'Good questions,' Bill noted, thinking hard and trying to make sense of it all.

'But now I know exactly where it all is,' Travis divulged. 'I saw it. It's in the blow hole.'

Bill suddenly clapped his hands together so hard that Janey nearly fell of her bucket.

'A blow hole!' he repeated. 'Of course, that would be a perfect hiding place for treasure. They would have tipped it all in through the headland and it would have been protected by the tide!'

Janey waited until he'd stopped cheering. 'Bill, can I ask you something?'

'Yeah, sure. Shoot.'

'Are you the Booty Bill that Travis once told me about? And is your name perhaps something to do with "booty" as in treasure, and not as in the boots you might wear on your feet?'

Bill lit another cigarette. 'It's true. I've made my name, my fame and my fortune from salvaging treasure in these parts over the years. That's why I'm particularly pissed off…' – he shouted the words 'pissed off' in Travis's direction – '…that my brother here didn't let me in on his secret foray.'

'Hear hear, that makes two of us,' Janey added.

Travis held up his hands. 'In my own defence, I have to say that I was still in search of, and not actually in possession of, said treasure at that point, so any secret foray was entirely speculative.'

Bill and Janey glared at him.

'Okay, so what do we do now?' Janey asked. 'I mean, how do we salvage it and claim our reward. What's next?'

'Ah, yes, the official bit. Once you have located it, you then have report it to the authorities.'

Travis looked immediately alarmed. 'Whoa! Who said anything about reporting it?'

'Erm... because it's the right thing to do?' Janey suggested.

'Because it's the *only* thing to do,' Booty Bill insisted. 'And because the last time I checked, the bank won't let you deposit pieces of eight into your savings account.'

Travis looked at them both incredulously. Handing it over certainly hadn't been in his plan. He knew these coins would be worth a fortune on the black market and in the collectables trade.

Bill continued. 'When I found the *Santa Maria* off the coast of St Marten in the summer of seventy four, I went straight to the coroner in good faith to report that I had identified the ship and her treasure trove. In accordance with the *Treasure Act Code of Practice*, I then applied for the rights to salvage and negotiate my share of the haul.'

Janey was super impressed. 'Oh wow! You mean there's actually a code for finding treasure?'

This was sounding more like the *Pirates of the Caribbean* to her every minute.

Travis rolled his eyes. 'Oh, for heaven's sake! Aren't they supposed to be more like guidelines?'

Bill, who considered the matter of salvaging treasure a very serious matter, ignored them and continued his tale.

'All that the *Santa Maria* had been carrying when she went down in a hurricane in 1681 had been well documented, but as I was the only one who knew exactly where she lay, that gave me leverage to negotiate my fee. Do you see?'

'And where is all the treasure from the *Santa Maria* now?' Janey asked him, fascinated by the whole story and this incredible insight.

'The entire haul, including the canons and the masthead, are now in the Nautical Museum,' Booty told her, proudly.

'And so how did you get a fair price for your part in finding the treasure?' she urged.

'It was valued independently and I was awarded fifty percent. I had to front my own salvage costs, but considering the wreck was in their coastal waters and it had belonged to the government in the first place, I felt fifty–fifty was a fair and generous split.'

Janey nodded enthusiastically, her eyes as big as saucers. In their situation, she guessed fifty percent of a fortune split three ways was still going to be a huge amount of money. This was *so* exciting. This was, without doubt, the most exciting thing that had ever happened to her; that assumption being based on the fact that being a castaway and being kidnapped was more on the traumatic side of things rather than the exciting.

Travis listened to all of this with an expression of despair on his face.

'Okay,' Janey continued to enthuse, 'so let's see if I understand this right. We need to salvage the treasure and then report it to the coroner on Tortola, keeping the location of our haul a secret, so that we have leverage to get permission to claim an even split from the owner?'

'Exactly!' Bill seemed satisfied that she'd understood the Code.

'And who owns the island, do you know?' Janey asked, looking at Travis for this information, while secretly hoping it might be Sir Richard Branson, as he had an island in the BVIs and she'd always wanted to meet him.

Travis was still frowning, his initial excitement dampened by the complications of the Code.

'It's part of the BVIs, so it's the Queen, I guess?' he answered flatly.

Janey bit the inside of her lip anxiously, wondering how on earth they would go about gaining permission to salvage treasure in the Virgin Islands from Buckingham Palace.

'Okay.' Travis stood up, as if concluding their discussions. 'So our mission is to salvage the coins and take them to a new secret hiding place known only to us. Any suggestions on where that place could be, Boots?'

Bill shook his head. 'I see a problem concerning safety rather than salvage. I mean, look what happened yesterday. Do you really think that a killer pirate on the loose is going to let us back on that island when he finds out you are still alive and that you know exactly where he has hidden the treasure?'

Janey's buoyant mood dissipated through the hull when she realised that Bill was right and this was actually a very dangerous operation with the killer pirate still at large.

Travis sat down on his bucket again. 'Yes, we have to be careful. He escaped custody so that he could kill me, and he very nearly succeeded. I have also been led to believe that given the chance, he would also kill you too, Janey.'

He saw the colour suddenly drain out of Janey's newly sun-kissed face as she gasped at this bit of information.

'Why does he want to kill me when I'm not even testifying against him?'

'According to the police, you gave a statement supporting my evidence. And if you hadn't left the island when you did, they'd have certainly offered you witness protection.'

Janey thought about that for a moment. 'Well, luckily, the fugitive pirate still doesn't know I'm back. So I'll just have to be sure to keep a low profile until he's recaptured.'

'And that's just another reason why I suggested to you this morning that you might wanna' stay at my place,' Travis insisted, hoping for a second shot at having her stay close with him.

Janey laughed. 'What, so you could look after me? Well, thanks but no thanks. Because if I'm number two on his hit list and you're number one, I'd probably be a lot safer at my hotel.'

'Did you check in under your own name?' Bill asked her.

'Well, of course I did.'

'Okay, then maybe you should stay at my place instead?' Bill suggested.

She looked first at Travis and then back at Bill. 'And how many bedrooms do you have?'

She heard Travis laugh, which he quickly tried to disguise as a cough.

Bill shrugged. 'I dunno? Ten, I think, but it could be more.'

Janey's eyes widened. 'Well, okay, if you have the space, then I'd love to.'

# Chapter Sixteen

Janey checked out of the hotel and moved into Bill's place as soon as they got back to Antigua. He lived in a beautiful low-rise sprawling villa in an elevated position overlooking both the Caribbean Sea and the marina. The entrance to his estate was gated and the driveway was long and winding. At the top of the peninsula, the views of St Johns and Nelson's Dockyard were breathtaking.

Janey noticed only one spot higher than Bill's house and that was The Fort itself, a popular visitor attraction, but you'd have certainly needed to look through binoculars or a telescope from the battlements in order to see exactly who was sitting on Bill's open deck verandas that ran along the entire length of his house, where there were comfortable chairs, hammocks, and tables for outdoor living. She was quite taken aback with it all. It was all so, well, unexpectedly fabulous.

Bill showed her an entire wing of the house that he said he didn't ever use except for when his family came over from The States.

'Help yourself to whichever bedroom suits you best,' he told her.

She chose a spacious and airy room with a set of French doors that opened straight out onto the decking with a good view of the marina and *The Mermaid* and the *Salva Vida's* moorings.

She wandered around the room for a while, enjoyed lying starfish-like across the big cool comfortable bed, and then freshened up in the most beautiful en-suite bathroom before she unpacked the few things she'd brought with her, hung them in the wardrobe to de-crease, and then chose a light cotton jumpsuit to wear. After which, she went in search of the kitchen. She found it by following the sound of men's voices.

Travis had just arrived. He'd previously gone back to his beach house to change. He'd brought takeaway pizzas with him and a couple of bottles of wine and he was chatting away to Bill. Janey noted how he was clean shaven, for a change. He was wearing brown leather flip-flops, loose fitting denim shorts, and a short-sleeved white linen shirt that coordinated perfectly with the white linen gauze dressing on his head. He looked cool and tanned and managed to carry off the casual but stylish look effortlessly.

'I love your house,' she told Bill, as the men acknowledged her.

She kissed him on the cheek. He too had shaved.

'Have you always lived here?'

He shook his head and laughed. 'Heavens, no. I bought it with my salvage royalties back in 1975. From a rock star, no less.'

'Really? Who?'

'No, not *The Who*, but someone who is, shall we say, of that same ilk and era.'

Janey's eyes were wide open with curiosity. She looked at Travis for a clue while Bill's back was turned, but Travis just grinned at her.

'Anyway, I'm gonna leave you kids to enjoy your pizza,' Bill told them. 'I have some stuff to do in town. I'll be a couple of hours so do behave yourselves.'

Realising she was about to be left alone with Travis, Janey suddenly felt herself perspiring.

Travis wrapped the neck of the wine bottle in a cloth and dumped it into a cooler, then picked up two glasses. 'Shall we go eat outside,' he suggested. 'I got a margarita and a pepperoni. You do like pizza, right?'

'Who doesn't like pizza?' she remarked, scooping up the boxes and following him.

Travis laughed. 'Actually, I don't think *The Who* do like pizza, but I know for sure that Eric Clapton does.' He poured two large glasses of golden chardonnay and handed one to Janey.

Her jaw dropped. 'Really? Eric Clapton? Wow!'

Raising his glass, Travis looked deeply into her eyes and asked, 'So, what are we drinking to?'

His eyes had darkened in a way that made her almost breathless. She emboldened herself and pondered the question for rather longer than was polite.

'How about being reunited?' he suggested to help her out.

'Actually, I was just going to say let's drink to the treasure hunt.'

She chinked her glass against his and they both took a sip of their wine. They sat out on the terrace, enjoying the warm mimosa-scented breeze from the garden while devouring their slices of pizza. Their conversation was carefully steered to cover topics such as the upcoming trial, the killer pirate who was still on the loose, their castaway island, its network of caves, his boat and her renovation and repair, about all boats in general, and about how Janey should really learn to scuba dive. Only when they had exhausted all these topics and started on their second bottle of wine, did they talk about anything that might be deemed personal.

Janey bravely broached the subject.

'Travis, I want to ask you something about the day we parted and I flew back to Scotland.'

Travis looked at her through the pale straw coloured wine in his glass. His blue eyes, slightly creased at the corners, encouraged her to continue but almost crushed her resolve to keep things simple as far as he was concerned.

'You sent me away…' she said quietly. 'I laid my heart on my sleeve that day at the hospital and you pretty much told me that you weren't interested. '

He looked pained. 'I know and I'm sorry, but now you know the truth, right?'

She shrugged. 'Do I? I don't honestly know what to believe. It's hard to trust you when it seems there are now two versions of the truth. Were you really trying to keep me away from the treasure, or heroically out of harm's way, I wonder?' Her voice sounded hardened by her cynicism.

'I wanted to keep you safe, Janey. I'd agreed to be the key witness in a murder trial and that placed you in danger. I had no choice. That's why I wanted you on the next plane off Antigua.'

She shrugged. 'So why didn't you just explain it to me like that at the time?'

He laughed. 'Ha, yeah, like that would have worked!'

She took another sip of wine.

*Okay, he was right about that as there's no way she'd have gone.*

But it still sounded to her like he hadn't expected her to come back and now he was just telling her exactly what he thought she wanted to hear. She tipped the last bit of wine into her mouth and put the glass down.

Travis lifted the bottle from the ice bucket.

'Oh, no. No more for me, thanks. You finish it. I know the night is still young but I'm feeling rather tired. Jet lag, I suppose. So, I'll see you at the marina in the morning?'

'Okay, sure. Jet lag. I hear that's really awful and that's why I stick to boats.' He stood up to slide open the heavy glass door into the house and then he leaned forward slightly, as if he might be expecting a goodnight peck on the cheek.

Janey slid passed him and avoided it.

At a safe distance, she turned to see his look of disappointment. 'Goodnight, Travis.'

'Goodnight, Janey.'

## Chapter Seventeen

A short while later, Travis was back at his beach house, pouring himself a large measure of rum. He could hardly believe that Janey was back on Antigua. Of course he was delighted to see her again, but he was also horrified, because she'd actually refused to believe that she was in any real danger. Instead, she'd chosen to be seriously pissed off with him for not including her in his plans to find the treasure, when he'd honestly had only her best interest at heart.

He hated how women over-thought this kinda stuff and then missed what was going on right in front of their faces. The pirate killer was on the loose and he was trying to kill them. It should have been obvious to her what was going on here. It was totally frustrating.

Thankfully, he felt she was safe at Booty's. The place was like a fortress.

He'd noticed that she still wasn't wearing a ring on her engagement finger, but as it had been stolen from her and she'd only been home a week, that didn't necessarily mean she wasn't still engaged. Perhaps he could persuade Bill to try to find out?

She had looked amazing tonight. When she'd walked into the kitchen in that slinky outfit, his heart had beat so fast that he thought he was actually in danger of having a bloody heart attack. And her perfume – what was that? Pure bloody pheromone or something?

The three of them had agreed to meet up again tomorrow at the private marina, to discuss a way forward with the treasure situation. He was of the opinion that they should immediately salvage it from the blow hole, because for all they knew, if the pirates had help from others with a vested interest, they could be planning to move it somewhere else.

Booty knew all there was to know about treasure salvage, but he was all about caution and following that bloody code. And Janey, as much as she liked a bit of adventure, liked to play by the rules and so wasn't really a code breaker.

His initial euphoria over finding the treasure now hung over his head like a bad hangover.

Tonight, rum was absolutely required so he settled into his armchair and poured himself another. He thought again about Janey. He imagined himself going over to Booty's place, scaling the walls, climbing up onto the veranda and sneaking into her bedroom, where he would whisk her into his arms and make love to her. A romantic notion but, of course, one that in real life would no doubt get him arrested.

Romantic notions aside, his exhausted body simply wouldn't allow for it. His head ached horribly, the staples holding his scalp together stung and now felt far too tight. His shoulder throbbed and it was difficult for him to find a comfortable way to either sit or lie down. He felt like he'd been through a war, which he supposed he had.

After he'd slugged back the last dreg of rum in his glass and placed it down on his desk, his eyelids became so heavy that he couldn't keep them open any longer, and within a few seconds of closing them, he had fallen soundly asleep.

He woke sometime later to a loud banging on his door.

*What time was it?*

*It was still dark, so was it late or very early?*

*Was it the killer pirate here to kill him?*

Travis leapt from his chair and took hold of his baseball bat propped against the wall. He stole over to the window without switching on the light. He peeped through the slats to see a shape at the door.

Whoever it was knocked again, more urgently this time. Then he heard a familiar voice. It was a woman's voice. He put down the bat and opened the door.


When Janey woke early the next morning in her luxurious bedroom, the sun was casting lines of white light across her face through the gaps in the curtains. She'd had a wonderful night's sleep and was looking forward to the day ahead immensely. She stretched herself lazily and felt ridiculously glad to be back here in the Caribbean now that she was properly rested and the jet lag had abated.

They were planning to meet up on Bill's boat again this morning, to discuss what to do about the coins. He'd also promised to give her a lesson in scuba diving. What a decadent lifestyle this was. Sun, sea, boats, and treasure hunting. It was a heady mix.

Realising she was ravenously hungry, she showered quickly, tied back her misbehaving hair into a ponytail, then dressed in shorts and a vest top, under which she wore her bikini.

As she entered the kitchen, she could see Booty sitting outside on the veranda. The table was set for breakfast and he was staring at his laptop. His brow was furrowed and his expression perplexed. When he saw her, he folded the laptop closed.

'Good morning, Janey. Tea? I just made a fresh pot.'

Janey accepted and sat down. There were delicious looking bread rolls and butter and jam and a bowl of sliced tropical fruits on the table. He poured her tea from the pot into a cup with a saucer.

'Help yourself to breakfast,' he smiled at her warmly. 'If you'd like eggs, I can rustle you some up?'

Clearly, Booty Bill lived like a colonial gentlemen up here on the hill, which you just wouldn't know about him based on seeing him in his oily overalls down at the marina, where he ran the fuel depot.

'No, I'm fine, thank you. This looks great. Any news yet of the killer pirate?' She'd assumed he'd been keeping up with news on the Internet.

Bill shook his head. 'Nothing so far. The coastguard is still out looking for him, of course, but he's likely gone to ground. I've been doing a bit of research on the silver reales, and I'm afraid I've come across another problem that could be a deal-breaker, regarding the salvage of the coins.'

She looked up from her tea cup. 'Oh, that sounds serious.'

'Yes, it is. Remember we discussed ownership?'

Janey nodded. 'We thought they might belong to the UK.'

'Well, yes. The island is British but the coins are definitely Spanish, and even after all these years, the Kingdom of Spain is still legally the rightful owner.'

Janey still did not fully understanding the implications.

Bill continued to explain. 'You see, in all the cases where the treasure is Spanish, it has always been immediately confiscated by the Kingdom of Spain and no reward has ever been awarded. It's not right, and it's not by the Code, but that's just the way it is.'

'No reward … ever?' Janey repeated.

'No. But it gets worse because it seems that even salvagers who've acted properly have been successfully prosecuted.'

'Prosecuted? For what?'

'For disturbing the treasure.'

'Oh, my goodness! So it looks like Travis might be right. I mean, about us keeping things to ourselves?'

'Not really, because those who've been caught selling Spanish booty on the black market have been hunted down by powerful international lawyers, caught, and then fined millions of dollars.'

'Millions of dollars…' Janey murmured like a faint echo.

'Or they go to jail for a very long time.'

*Fined? Prosecuted? Jail?*

'There's a case ongoing in Florida right now,' he explained, 'to do with a Spanish wreck discovered just off the Bahamas, and it doesn't look good for the poor buggers who found it all.'

'We have to break this news to Travis,' Janey exclaimed.

'Look, you stay here and enjoy your breakfast, and I'll go over to his beach house now. I'll explain it to him just the way I've explained it to you,' Bill offered. 'That way, we can meet up on the *Salva Vida* later, once he's had a chance to calm down, and decide between us how to proceed.'

Janey agreed. Like Bill, she didn't expect Travis to take this very well at all.


Bill knocked on the door of Travis's beach house and was surprised when the door was answered by Honey, who greeted him with a piece of toast in her hand.

'Hi, sweetheart, I gotta talk to Travis. It's important.'

Honey yelled, 'Travis, Booty is here.'

Travis emerged from the bathroom with a towel around his waist.

'What is it, Boots? What's so important that it couldn't wait till we met up at the marina?'

'I couldn't wait. I've been up all night checking and double checking everything.'

'You want some coffee?' Travis asked him.

Honey wandered off into the kitchen. Travis insisted that Booty sat down.

'I've discovered a much bigger problem concerning the coins,' Bill began.

'What coins?' said Honey, coming out of the kitchen with a pot of coffee.

Travis's eyes shot up in alarm, indicating that perhaps he might be a little more discreet.

'What coins?' she repeated.

'Bit coins,' Travis told her. 'It's a virtual currency on the Internet that we are investing in, isn't that right, Boots?'

Bill caught on immediately and nodded enthusiastically before returning to his concerns.

'Well, you know how I'd explained about securing those coins, you know, using the proper procedures…?

Travis laughed nervously. 'Yeah, well, nobody said investing in bit coins was gonna be easy.'

'This problem is one of original ownership.'

'Right, I'm with you now… I think?'

'There is a prosecution case ongoing in Florida, between a well established… erm… bit coin trader and a, erm… Spanish owner. You can probably guess who is winning.'

'The Spanish!' Honey guessed, cheering and waving her hands in the air.

'That's absolutely right,' Bill confirmed, his eyes rolling over Honey's ample cleavage.

'And you are saying this will affect us because our coins are Spanish?' Travis questioned.

Bill nodded.

Travis scratched his chin and brooded on this point. If Booty said they had a problem with the treasure, then there was no doubt that they did.

Bill finished his coffee and stood up to leave. 'Look, Travis, I'm really sorry to bring this to your attention so early in the morning, but there's no point in you thinking there's gonna be a big commission when we hand them over, because I doubt there would be.'

'Then we won't hand them over,' Travis said quite categorically.

## Chapter Eighteen

'So, what's Honey doing back?' Booty asked Travis in a whisper, as they prepared the *Salva Vida* for leaving the marina. 'I thought you and her were over because you had the hots for madam over there?' They both glanced over at Janey, who was on the dock helping to load the diving gear.

'Well, apparently Honey was offered big bucks by the hotel to come back and cover for a dancer who is sick this week, Travis hissed.

Booty said, 'Arh,' and nodded. 'And she's staying at your place?'

'No. Not anymore,' Travis explained. 'So, there's no point in even mentioning that she was there last night to anyone.' He indicted towards Janey, who he knew would get the wrong idea, scuppering any chance he had of softening her mood towards him today.

Booty tapped the side of his nose to assure his friend of his absolute discretion.

'Is someone going to help me with these heavy tanks?' Janey yelled to them.


Once all the gear was on board, Booty, with all the authority of a boat captain, briefed them on the day's activities.

'Okay, I propose that this morning we head out to one of our beautiful Antiguan dive spots, where we have some fun teaching Janey here how to scuba dive.'

They set off around the coastline, with Travis keeping a keen eye open for any sign of pirates.

A short while later, in a cove over a shallow part of a reef they anchored up. Satisfied that they weren't likely to be observed or disturbed, three upturned buckets were placed on the deck. Bill said that was the cue for their pre-dive powwow and he wanted to brief them on basic dive safety and diving procedures.

Travis, who was visibly wound up with frustration about the treasure trove, vetoed Bill's talk.

'Okay, I'd like to suggest that after Janey's dive lesson this morning, we all go back to the blow hole pool, dive down to retrieve the coins and then stash them somewhere else until a later date.'

Bill raised his eyebrows. 'How late a date and where would we stash them?'

Travis shrugged. 'Until the time is right. Certainly until after the killer pirate has been recaptured and the trial is over. And, I dunno, somewhere known to only the three of us?'

'I have a couple of concerns with that plan,' Janey expressed. 'I think it's pretty risky for us to go anywhere near the blow hole cave while the pirate is still at large. Look what happened last time. As for removing the coins, if we get caught we could be implicated and indicted and I don't want to go to jail. Do you?'

'She's got a good point,' said Bill.

Travis looked a little deflated. 'Okay, then let's hear your suggestions?'

'Ladies first…' Bill insisted, happy to act as mediator.

Janey let out a long sigh while she was thinking about how best to present her proposal.

'Okay, as I've mentioned, I'm a bit worried about the pirate still being at large. The coastguard has had no success tracking him down and Bill thinks that he's gone to ground. But, we need him out of the picture so we can go and get our coins. I suggest we flush him out.'

Travis jerked his head up in surprise.

Bill looked a little stunned. 'Flush him out?'

'Yes. We believe he's watching the island, particularly the blow hole cave, so we should go back there with a plan to trap him, so he can be recaptured and face trial.'

Travis started laughing. 'That's the craziest plan I ever heard – but I do think it might work!'

'What do you suggest? That we lure him onto the island and steal his boat?' Booty asked.

Janey shook her head. 'He knows the island too well and he could hide for a very long time in any of the caves there. I suggest we lure him inside the blow hole cave, blow up both exits so that the only access in or out of the cavern will be through the top, and then let the coastguard know that's exactly how they'll recapture him,' Janey explained.

Bill reeled on his upturned bucket. 'I hope you don't think I'm gonna let you two scallywags on my boat with explosives. And who the hell is going to light the charges anyway?'

'But it's also ingenious and, if we can pull it off,' Travis enthused, 'the pirate will be back in custody, the trial will go ahead as planned, and we can return to take our time salvaging the coins.'

'Bloody crazy, that's what this is,' Bill grumbled. 'And bloody dangerous too!'

Janey beamed at him while she basked in his approval. It felt exciting to be having adventures. She felt her blood was pounding through her veins and her heart was pumping like a steam train engine. She felt alive once more, just like when they'd been castaways together on the island.

Booty passed out the dive gear for Janey's first lesson. 'This is a perfect place for you to learn how to dive, Janey. It's a nursery reef, where the water is warm and shallow and there are lots of tiny fish and colourful plants for you to see. It's like an underwater garden down there.'

Despite his colourful description of the underwater scene, Janey looked apprehensively at the wetsuit he held out to her. Like many people, she had a healthy respect for water and a real fear of drowning.

*What if her air supply failed?*

*Or if she sank down to the bottom with all the weight of this diving gear and couldn't get back up again?*

Bill saw her hesitation. 'You still want to do it, don't you?'

She took the suit from him. 'Yes, of course.'

She stripped down to her bikini and was amused to see that Travis had sneaked an amorous peek at her as she did so. She pulled on the suit and pulled up the zipper.

Travis was sorting out his own dive gear and removing his head gauze. Again, she found herself wincing at the strip of black staples in his scalp.

The three of them donned inflatable jackets with air tanks and breathing regulators attached to them. They wore fins on their feet and what felt like very heavy weight belts around their waists.

Janey wondered how she would ever be able to swim wearing all of this cumbersome gear.

Finally, she was handed a face mask and a snorkel.

Bill explained the hand signals they would use underwater for communication.

Travis, she learned, was already a qualified diver and Bill had been his instructor too.

In the warm shallow water just off the beach, she was shown how to clear her face mask if it flooded with water, and how to take the mouthpiece out and put it back in her mouth again.

'Breathe just as you would on the surface, slowly, but through the regulator.'

They practiced this a few times and then Bill took her to where it was a few metres deeper so she could practice clearing the water pressure on her ears by squeezing her nose and blowing out.

It felt strange to be breathing underwater, but she knew that this was going to be the only way she would ever get to see the coins in situ, so she would brave it out and follow Bill's instructions.

Once she'd given them the 'okay' sign with her thumb and forefinger, Travis led them across a shallow reef, pointing out an octopus hiding in the colourful coral and a tiny cute sea horse clinging with its tail to a swaying piece of sea grass; all things that were so well camouflaged in their environment that she would have missed them otherwise.

Bill kept to the back of their little group, keeping his expert eyes on Janey.

The dive on the reef lasted almost an hour and Janey loved every minute of it.

Back on the *Salva Vida*, in his tight-fitting wetsuit, she had to admit that Travis looked even sexier than usual. The suit emphasised his broad shoulders and his slim waist and the tight roundness of his buttocks. Not that she was staring or anything.

He noticed her looking and grinned.

She looked away quickly, suddenly realising she was playing his game.

Then she thought she heard him groan. It was only the slightest murmur but it made her turn to look at him again. He was trying to pull the wetsuit off his injured shoulder. She could see where the bullet hole had been; the skin looked red and stretched.

'Here, Travis, let me help you with that?'

She stood behind him and helped him to peel away the neoprene fabric down to his waist.

Then he turned to face her. His voice had lowered to almost a whisper as his fingers toyed with her zipper. 'How about I help you get out of yours?'

Bill busied himself with an air tank, suddenly venting it off noisily.

Janey took a step back in earnest. 'Erm, thanks, but I think I've got it.'

It was time for lunch. They had brought a picnic. Janey had helped haul an ice box into the back of Bill's jeep that morning and they'd stopped off at the shops on the way down to the marina to buy bottled water, packets of sandwiches, and snacks. Travis's contribution was a cool box full of barbecue food.

So they sat on deck in the hot sunshine, being rocked by the boat, listening to waves lapping against the hull, eating lunch and quietly contemplating; at least that's what Janey was doing. She was thinking how smug she felt about being out on the Caribbean Sea on this perfect day of blue skies and blue sea, when she could have so easily been sitting in her stuffy office in Edinburgh right now, if her life hadn't been so dramatically changed by circumstance.

Her thoughts were broken by the sound of Travis breaking her open a can of ice-cold cola.

He handed it to her. 'How do you feel about heading out to the blow hole this afternoon and looking at some treasure?' he asked.

Janey immediately agreed. Now that she knew how to dive it was all she could think about.

'I'd love that.' She looked to Bill. 'Can we?'

Bill looked a little apprehensive. 'Could be risky if the fugitive's about?'

Travis laughed. 'If he is then we'll put Janey's plan into action and capture the bastard.'

They made their foray back to the island carefully and stealthily. They skirted the coastline at a safe distance, looking out for any suspicious vessel that might be hidden in a cove, or for anything that might indicate that the killer pirate was back ashore.

Eventually, satisfied that they were alone, they dropped anchor at low tide in an ingress near to the beach and they went ashore in their wetsuits.

Getting from the boat to the blow hole cavern proved to be quite an ordeal in the heat with the sun overhead as they had to carry their air tanks, their deflated jackets and the rest of their dive equipment up the beach and across the rocks.

Travis went into the cave first. Janey encouraged Bill to go in next and she followed. Safely inside, the space opened up in front of them and the natural light from the blow hole flooded down, lighting up stalactites and stalagmites and reflecting down into the round pool of blue water.

Travis indicated that they should wait until he scouted the cavern to be sure it was safe.

Once the all clear was given, Bill immediately rushed over to the pool that he'd heard so much about from Janey and Travis, first looking down into it and then tipping back his head and looking up in wonder at the sky above.

'Yep, it's a blow hole all right,' he said, 'and a perfect place to hide treasure!'

He knelt down and tasted the water. 'It's a combination of freshwater from the underground springs and saltwater from the sea – an ideal mix for protecting against corrosion over the years.'

'So that's why the dates were so clearly visible on the coins?' Janey noted.

Bill nodded. 'They'd be gleaming like they were minted only yesterday.'

She was beyond excitement but also incredibly nervous. Diving into a deep underwater cave system was a big deal. She was trembling like a jellyfish as Travis helped her to fasten on her jacket and tank again.

'You'll be fine. We'll look after you,' he promised.

'Our bottom time will only be five minutes,' Bill told them, looking at his dive watch.

They waded into the shallow part of the pool. In the middle there was a perfectly circular and sheer drop to the bottom of the sparkling abyss. The water was warm on the surface but felt considerably colder as they descended. Janey kept her thoughts focussed only on what she would see at the bottom rather than how scared she felt at reaching it. In the clear water, with the light cascading down from above, she thought they looked like three ethereal shadows suspended in blue space. When Janey looked up she could no longer see the surface, and when she looked down there was nothing below. She felt herself panic a little and she suddenly realised she was breathing far too fast. She could hear herself sucking air noisily through her regulator and blowing it out again in a stream of bubbles.

Bill gave the signal to halt and then he maintained eye contact with her until her breathing had slowed. Only once she had assured him she was feeling better, using the 'okay' signal, did they continue their descent into what felt to Janey like the bowels of the earth.

She felt completely weightless, like an astronaut floating around in space. Then suddenly the bottom of the pool appeared and she said 'Wow!' while forgetting she couldn't speak under water.

Her voice came out as a throaty growl in a stream of air bubbles. She looked at Travis and gave him the thumbs-up with excitement.

He took his regulator out of his mouth to give her the full width of his grin.

The three of them hovered just a few inches over the coins, which lay in the sand just as Travis had described them: like layers of shiny silver fish scales.

They were careful not to kick up sand with their fins or to disturb the scene in any way.

Travis took photographs and then he handed the camera to Bill, who took some more.

Janey hovered in a skydiver position, gazing down at the centuries-old coins just inches from her grasp. When Bill gave her the nod, she reached slowly out with her hand to take one. The coin filled her palm. It shimmered in her hand and looked to be as new as the day it had been minted.

On one side, stamped into the silver, was a coat of arms. She flipped it over to see the dated side: 1732. Along with the date on this side of the coin there was an image incorporating a crown with two circles flanked by two pillars ornately wrapped with scrolls.

*Was this why the coin, the universal currency of the time, was also known as the pillar dollar?*

She slipped the coin back into its special place in the fish scale pattern.

She felt elated. Today she had touched history. She had held something in her hand that had not been touched by another human hand in centuries. It felt like she had touched a gap in the fabric of time itself and that feeling alone was a treasure. This was a very special moment and one she would undoubtedly remember all her life.

As soon as they surfaced, Travis was already thinking ahead to the salvage operation. 'Okay, we'll need to bring about twenty more hessian sacks with us next time to hold all the coins.'

'And a pulley system to bring them all to the surface,' Bill added, as they unburdened themselves of tanks and jackets and weights.

Janey giggled. It wasn't every day she saw pirate treasure in an old cave on a Caribbean island.

On the beach, on their way back to the boat, Janey drew out their mission plan in the wet sand with a stick. The plan showed the lay of the cave in the headland and showed the two entrances.

'This is entrance number one where Travis will lay his charges.' She circled it with her stick. 'And this is entrance two, where Bill will blow the first charge as soon as I give the signal from the headland that the pirate is in the cave. On hearing the explosion, Travis will immediately detonate his charges, sealing the cave and capturing the pirate. Everyone okay with this plan?'

Travis nodded. 'Yep, seems simple enough to me.'

Bill looked horrified. 'And when do we do this, exactly?'

'There's no exactly, I'm afraid,' Janey explained. 'It's whenever the pirate turns up. But I do think we should make a start on preparing the explosives. Travis, did you get a good look at the entrances and the best places to lay the charges?'

'Yes, I did. I know exactly where to place them and how many we'll need.'

Bill looked astonished. 'Being with you two is like being in the bloody commandos!'

# Chapter Nineteen

It was early evening and the sun was low in the sky. In the Caribbean it never took very long for the sun to go down over the horizon and the sunsets were always spectacular, leaving a pitch-black backdrop for the millions of stars that popped onto the scene like tiny camera flashes.

Janey helped to get all the scuba gear aboard and then she excused herself. She needed time to think. She climbed up onto the roof of the wheelhouse and stretched out. Feeling both tired and reflective, she looked up at the timeless stars and constellations above her that looked like tiny silver coins littering the sky. She thought about the centuries-old legend of the missing silver coins, except they were no longer truly missing, and if Travis was right about them, they hadn't been missing for some time. Had the pirate gang, who had been guarding and squabbling over them, known that the Spanish government would have immediately confiscated the coins and offered no reward? Is that why they'd never moved them or sold them on?

It made sense. How would it be possible to profit from selling such a well-documented piece of history? How exactly would you account for thousands of silver coins suddenly flooding the open market or, indeed, the black market, and even bringing down silver prices?

Surely to do so would arouse suspicion and even warrant an official inquiry?

It seemed that salvaging the treasure was a romantic notion but not a practical one.

Surely Travis must know this?

If not, then he really hadn't thought it through. Did he really think it was going to be as simple as in *Treasure Island* or when Bill famously salvaged his treasure off Saint Marten?

Travis had got the barbeque going. It was a metal drum type that cleverly clipped on to the aft of the boat. The smoke from the hot charcoal curled and blew away on the evening breeze. He had his cool box open and he was bringing out hot dogs and burgers. He also had bread rolls and a jar of what he said was his own brand of mustard chutney, and beer, of course, to wash the meal down.

The smell of the smoky food cooking brought Janey down from the top of the wheelhouse.

She helped him with preparations where she could, although Travis always liked to take control of the kitchen. She split the rolls while he chopped a few onions and tomatoes to throw together a salsa. When they sat down to eat, they avoided talk of coins. Instead they chatted about diving.

Booty told Janey that he'd been impressed with her performance as a diver.

'You should consider getting yourself certified,' he told her.

She laughed. Obviously getting certified here in the Caribbean wasn't the same sort of certified that Mark had suggested to her the last time she'd seen him, when he'd informed her she was completely mad for leaving him.

*Yes, she'd been mad all right.*

'Bill's right,' Travis agreed, between mouthfuls of hotdog. 'You should think about taking an open water course before you leave the Caribbean.'

Janey didn't answer immediately as she'd just taken a bite out of her own hotdog but she took a moment to digest his words. He'd caught her off guard again, just like the last time, with his dismissive tone. To say it hurt was an understatement.

She took a sip of beer and thought about how to respond when there was a loud thud and a cracking sound. Janey immediately looked over in alarm at the barbecue. Had it exploded?

In the same split second, Travis launched himself at both her and Bill, dragging them to the floor of the deck. He landed heavily, knocking the breath out of both of them. His lips were right next to Janey's ear when he said, 'It's gunfire. Keep your head down.'

'The pirate!' Janey gasped, knowing that it could be no one else.

Bill rolled away from them towards the wheelhouse and made moves to start the engine.

Travis hauled anchor.

Another shot ran out. Where the bullet went, no one knew, but thankfully no one was hit.

'Go!' Travis yelled to Bill.

The *Salva Vida*'s powerful engines roared into life and they made their getaway using the jagged coves and outcrops of rock and headland to disguise their movements. Then, once they felt they'd made enough distance, they kept their lights off and the engine silent.

'We'd be better staying put here until the morning,' Bill advised.

'Yeah,' Travis agreed. 'If we can't see him then he can't see us so he won't risk making a move.'

'And what will we do then?' Janey asked in a shaky voice, her enthusiasm for the plan to capture the pirate now at an all time low.

'We have to think up a plan to get him inside the cave,' Travis told her, with a glint of mischief in his eye.

It seemed there was nothing quite like being shot at to ignite his adventurous side.


At the first sign of morning light, there was no sign of the pirate's boat so Bill took the *Salva Vida* as close into the beach as he dared. Once Travis and Janey were ashore, he took the boat out again to a point where he would be able to make a quick exit if one was needed.

Janey and Travis made their way to the headland, where they would be afforded a better view for their lookout. The pirate killer had retreated, but they knew he had to be somewhere nearby and they didn't want him spotting them before they spotted him.

'Remember to look out for our key ingredients, Janey,' Travis told her, as they scrabbled across rocks and shale to the entrance to the blow hole cave.

He'd already pocketed the charcoal from the previous night's barbeque and now he was picking up volcanic rocks.

'These rocks are tinged with elemental sulphur,' he told her, as enthusiastically as if he'd found the right herb for his latest culinary creation.

Janey popped another couple of coconuts in her backpack and told him she was 'onto it'.

Entrance number one of the two entrances to the blow hole cave was where bats had once colonised, and where Travis knew they'd find all the dried guano they needed: the final ingredient for any decently constructed explosive device.

Once they were in position, Travis used his torch to signal Bill, who was still on the boat.

Bill flashed back that all was well, so Travis and Janey sat down and started assembling their fire power. An hour later, they were fully equipped and had packed their grenades around each of the two cave entrances. They used five on each, one on each side and three over the top, to cause a collapse that would block the cave. They were also careful to place stones to disguise the charges.

Then it was the waiting game.

They signalled Bill to come ashore.

This was the part of the plan that Bill had trouble with, especially as he'd seen what had happened to *The Mermaid* but, somehow, Travis had managed to convince him that the pirate would be more interested in chasing the people who were trying to take the coins than in blowing up his boat. Janey had noticed that Travis had his fingers crossed the whole time he said this.

However, Bill must have believed him because now he was coming ashore to take up his position near to the second cave entrance.

They waited and waited and then, as the sun came up fully over the horizon, so did a small boat.

They watched the boat get closer and closer. It was headed into the next cove.

Janey waited with bated breath as she watched through her binoculars for Bill's next signal.

Then there it was – a few flashes from his torch to say that it was indeed 'their' pirate.

'We have the go signal,' Janey told Travis.

Travis cheered under his breath as Janey lay flat down on the rocks next to him with adrenaline now coursing through her veins like hot lava. Her heart was beating almost out of her chest. She could feel the heat from Travis's body radiating into hers and she could smell the masculine scent of his sweat. She looked at him, fixated on the tiny beads of perspiration that had formed on his top lip, as he anticipated their next move.

A moment later there was a follow-up flash from Bill to say the pirate had entered the cave.

Travis made his move, scuttling down the rock as stealthily as he could to get to his position on the other side on the cave.

From her midpoint position between the two access points, Janey gave Bill the go ahead to light his fuses. One minute later came the explosion they had been waiting for. All she could see afterwards was a big cloud of dust rising up into the air.

She hoped Bill had made his escape but there was no way at that moment of knowing.

Then she made her way quickly to Travis, whose cue to light his fuses was the first explosion.

There was no doubt he'd heard it and several tonnes of rock being disturbed.

The second explosion happened quicker than she anticipated and she literally felt the ground move. It shook under her feet like a mini earthquake. Her breath came quick and fast as she hurled herself down from the headland to find Travis was covered, completely covered, in dust. He looked like he'd had a huge bag of flour emptied onto him.

He was laughing. 'Take that, yer pirate bastard!' he yelled, shaking his fist in the air.

'Aye, take that, you snivelling pirate pile of shite!' came Bill's ecstatic contribution, who appeared none the worse for his part, except for an equally thick layer of dust.

'Time to get back to the *Salva Vida* and radio the coastguard helicopter, I think?' Janey suggested.

It was late afternoon when they got back to the marina, and Bill suggested that Travis join them for cocktails and a meal at his house that evening to celebrate.

*Cocktails?* Janey suspected that Bill was trying to do a bit of matchmaking.

Travis said he'd love to and he offered to cook but Bill insisted that this was 'his treat'.

She was secretly pleased that Bill had invited Travis over because it was easier for her to feign disapproval, and to allow Bill set the scene for her and Travis to spend more time together, than it was to try to do it herself and risk being rejected, if Travis suddenly thought things were getting too complicated for his not-so-simple life.

Back at the house, looking through the few clothes she had hanging in the vast wardrobe, she felt she didn't have anything suitably impressive or stylish enough for cocktails in a rock star villa on such an auspicious Caribbean evening. So she decided to go into town to buy a new dress.

She'd noticed there were several batik-style boutiques on the landings and she was keen to have an excuse to explore these shops and their colourful clothes made in the local light and silky fabrics. So she grabbed her purse and took a wander down the hill.

The landings were a row of shops on the boardwalk next to the port. It was the place where all the big boats and the ships anchored up, so the shops there catered for the wealthy cruise line passengers by selling jewellery, trinkets and boutique clothing.

Janey peeped inquisitively into one of the shop windows and wondered if she could afford anything. It was then she set eyes on a gorgeous silk shift dress in a colourful flowery batik fabric and immediately loved it. She imagined herself wearing it, perhaps with a fresh tropical flower from the garden in her hair, sipping a cocktail as the sun went down on the veranda while deep in conversation with Travis.

Her imaginative scene was interrupted by a high-pitched voice her calling her name.

'Jayyynneee… is that you?'

Janey turned to see a woman with bronze-coloured legs that seemed to go on forever rushing towards her. She had shiny dark hair swinging behind her head in a high ponytail. She was wearing an incredibly short dress and fashionable high-heeled wedges.

She waved and smiled at Janey as if she knew her really well.

It was only when the woman removed her sunglasses that Janey recognised Honey.

'How are you, Janey?' she asked in her annoying lisp of a Latino accent.

'Erm, good, thanks. I'm good.'

'You are back on the island, no?' she squealed.

Janey nodded, thinking how stupidly obvious that was, and inhaled a warm waft of Honey's heavy perfume. 'Yes, I thought I needed another Caribbean vacation.'

'And have you seen my Travis, yes?'

'Yes, I have,' Janey said, feeling even more irritated. 'He told me you were in Florida, actually.'

Honey smiled. 'I was, but I came back, and he let me sleep in his bed last night because I arrived so late on the island. He is such a sweetie, no?' She laughed and swished her ponytail.

Janey tried to stay composed. 'Oh, well, it was very nice seeing you again, but I really have to go.'

Using the shop door to make her escape, Janey found herself inside the air-conditioned boutique. She gulped in the ice-cold air gratefully and shook her head to try to erase the awful porn-like images of Honey with Mark and then Honey with Travis and not to throw up.

A shop assistant dashed to her side. 'Can I help you, madam?'

Janey pointed to the dress in the window. 'Yes, I'll take that one, thank you.'

Back at the villa, she laid her beautiful batik cocktail dress on the bed and stared at it. It now seemed far too vibrant for her mood. She had been looking forward to this evening, spending time with Bill and Travis, going over their adventure, talking about the scary parts and enthusing about their bravado, but how could she bear to look at him now, to listen to his conversation, and to endure his playful flirtations when she knew that he had spent the previous night with a girl he had claimed he only kept on his arm to have a bit of fun with?

If she could have feigned a headache then she would have done. But it didn't seem fair to Bill, when he had been so kind to her and when tonight he had gone to such lengths to order in a celebration gourmet meal from an exclusive local catering company. She just couldn't do that to him.

So she made the decision to say nothing and to leave Antigua first thing in the morning.

She had been a fool thinking that coming here could have changed things between them. Travis was, indeed, the man she'd first thought he was: awful, rude, arrogant, a tourist hater and a womaniser. Why on earth she'd been taken in by him and allowed him to kiss her that way, even though she was an engaged woman on holiday with her fiancé at the time.

The gall of the man was incomprehensible.

He could keep his damned silver coins. *The Judas!*

She took a shower and tried to wash her gloom and her tears away. It didn't work. She towel dried her hair and stared critically at her naked reflection in the mirror. She ran her hands down the length of her body, over her small round breasts, her almost concave belly and her jutting hips. She'd always been slim but had understandably lost quite a bit of weight over the past few weeks. Travis had said on numerous occasions that she was too skinny – well that was because he clearly preferred women with voluptuous curves.

*What was she thinking?*

*She had never been his type.*

She tried to tease her normally straight hair into some sort of a style, but the crazy curls it had adopted in the humid Caribbean air made her efforts a pointless task. In frustration, she pulled it back instead, and rolled it into a chignon at the nape of her neck while allowing a couple of tendrils to fall at her cheekbones. She slipped into her new silk dress and her low-heel gold sandals and then joined Bill on the veranda. More than anything, she needed a drink.

It was a balmy night but there was a gentle breeze blowing in from the sea, giving a delightful respite from the heat of the day. In the pitch-black sky, stars were out in force and there was a tiny slice of moon, just enough to add a shimmer to the watery vista in front of them.

'You look very pretty tonight, Janey,' Bill told her, picking a pretty pink hibiscus flower from a bush overhanging the veranda and sliding the stem behind her right ear.

'And you look rather dashing,' she told him, determined to boost her mood for his benefit.

Bill was wearing linen trousers with a short-sleeved and collared shirt. It was the first time she'd seen him in anything other than his well-worn shorts and a grubby vest top.

'And the table looks so…' she enthused.

It was set with a table cloth, napkins, classy looking cutlery, glassware that twinkled in the candlelight and a bowl of tropical flowers.

'So very…'

'Romantic?' Bill suggested.

'Atmospheric!' she concluded.

'Travis should be here soon, but shall we have a drink while we wait?' he suggested.

He mixed them both a vodka martini.

Janey's heart sank at the thought that he might bring Honey along too.

She had just taken a sip from her glass when she saw Travis enter the room. Her heart leapt, thudding painfully into her rib cage. He was wearing light-coloured chino trousers and a pale blue shirt. He looked breathtakingly handsome indeed. She realised she was holding her breath and let it go once she saw that Honey wasn't with him.

He approached and gave Janey a kiss on her cheek. 'Mmmm… and you smell amazing,' he whispered in her ear as his mouth brushed past her hair.

She heard him inhale her scent and shivered, despite the heat.

He'd brought a very good bottle of champagne and he held it up for them to see while declaring, 'We have something big to celebrate!' He was beaming from ear to ear.

Janey drained her martini glass and braced herself, in case this was something to do with Honey's return.

'Well, come on, tell us. Don't keep us in suspense,' Bill urged.

'I've just come off the phone with the police. The pirate killer is in custody.'

Bill cheered. 'I hope they got him out just as the tide was in. The bastard deserved it.'

Travis popped the cork and charged three glasses with the foaming fizz. 'But even bigger news is the trial that was postponed is now back on. I've been told to be at court to testify at nine am tomorrow morning, which also means that by tomorrow afternoon we'll be back on the treasure trail again!'

Janey felt rather light-headed. This was all happening so fast and she needed food or she might keel over at any moment. She pondered over the news. If the trial was tomorrow and Travis was in court testifying, then he would need their support, so she should probably stay just one more day.

*It would be the right thing to do, whether he appreciated it or not.*

They raised their glasses high and toasted to a guilty verdict and a lengthy sentence for the killer pirate, after which Bill checked his watch and looked a little agitated.

'Where *is* the food I ordered? We should be having our canapés right now.'

Their conversation was then once again about the killer pirate, about the trial and about escalating piracy in the Caribbean. Travis had some strong opinions and advocated the death penalty for the lot of them. Janey, who was stoically against capital punishment, argued her point so vociferously that Travis began to feel a strong sense that she might have a problem with him this evening. Bill topped up their glasses, and told them both off for being overly confrontational. He suggested they change the subject to something a little lighter. So they glared at each other over small talk until Bill suddenly rushed off to answer the security intercom on the front gate.

'That's the food at last!' he said with some relief.

'You know, I think you might have had too much champagne tonight, Janey,' Travis told her bluntly as soon as Bill had left the veranda.

Janey was incensed. 'On the contrary, I don't think I've had enough. You, on the other hand, might want to curb your alcoholic intake just in case your girlfriend requires your attention in the bedroom again tonight.'

*Ha! There, she'd said it.*

She took a step back from him and wobbled a little on her heels. Travis instinctively reached out a hand to steady her but she shirked away from him.

'Arh, I should have guessed,' he said with sigh. 'You know that Honey came by my house last night.'

'Yes, because she told me, when actually I'd much rather have heard it from you. If you two are back together again then that's none of my business, but I do think you should know that Honey slept with my fiancé while you and I were marooned on the island, and that's why Mark and I split up.'

He looked genuinely taken aback by this. 'Really? You've split up?'

*Did he not listen to anything? She'd just told him that his girlfriend slept around.*

She let out a drunken hiccup and then a little champagne burp. 'Yes. I'm done with men. Done. Finito!' Then all of a sudden, she began to feel horribly queasy. 'I'm off to freshen up before dinner,' she told him as an excuse to dash for the bathroom.

She hurried inside and down the long corridor towards her room, hoping he hadn't seen her in tears. She passed one of the caterers in the corridor. He was dressed in whites and carrying a plate of canapés. He smiled at her. She noticed he had a gold tooth in his mouth and a tattoo on his neck, some kind of tribal design, peeking out of his collar. It looked strangely familiar to her.

Then she heard Bill saying, 'Set down the canapés here and please do serve the starter course in exactly fifteen minutes time; my guests are getting hungry.'

Janey reached the end of the corridor and her room and was about to push open the door when she felt someone pushing roughly into her from behind, and as she opened her mouth to object, she felt a hand swipe over her mouth with a cloth that smelled very strongly of something very nasty.

For a moment she felt as though she was choking and then everything went even more wobbly and her head fell back. She thought she might be floating horizontally a few feet above the floor but then realised she was being carried through the kitchen. She tried to kick her legs but her body wouldn't obey. She couldn't move at all but her eyes were wide open and she could see she was in the arms of a man. A man who wore a caterer's uniform.

Her head lolled against his chest and she was helpless to escape or even to scream for help.

A moment later she was being tossed into the back of a van. The last thing she saw as a bag was put over her head was another tribal tattoo.


Travis studied the canapés. He considered these tiny but tasty snacks a quandary for a hungry man with big hands and an even bigger appetite. He took one and popped it into his mouth.

It was delicious but he immediately wanted another.

Bill appeared a moment later with a clutch of champagne flutes refilled.

'I've made Bellinis. Where's Janey?'

'Taking an awful long time putting on her lipstick, or whatever it is that women do when they disappeared into their bathrooms. I think I'd best go and check on her,' Travis told him.

'I've noticed she's been sharp with both of us tonight. I hope you haven't upset her again.'

Travis looked a little guilty. 'I'm afraid if she's sulking, it's probably all my fault.'

Bill shook his head in dismay. 'Oh. So she found out that Honey-bun stayed at your place last night, did she? I promise it wasn't me who snitched on you.'

'I'll see if I can tempt her back to us with the promise of a Booty Bill Bellini.'

'It's the room right at the far end of the corridor,' Bill told him while popping a crab crouton into his mouth. 'Mmm, oh wow, these are rather tasty. If you are not back in five minutes all these canapés will be gone.'

Travis tapped on the door of Janey's room. There was no answer.

'Janey, come on, let's talk,' he called out. 'You must know how I feel about you?'

*She was being unbelievably stubborn. This was so typical of her, even if frustratingly, it was one of the things he loved about her.*

'Janey, I want you to know that I didn't sleep with Honey the other night, and I was going to ask you to stay that day at the hospital, but I was afraid that if I did, you would be in danger and I couldn't do that to you. You have to believe me. Janey? Janey?'

He spent a while trying to coax her to join them but she would neither answer him nor come out of her room. He decided that, as she had been rather drunk, that she must have fallen asleep and so he was probably best to let her get some rest.

Reluctantly, he returned to join Bill and help polish off the canapés.

'I don't know what's keeping the first course,' Bill declared. 'I told them to serve up in fifteen minutes and it's way past that. I suppose I'll have to go see if I can hurry the kitchen along a bit.'

Travis downed his Bellini in one gulp and said he was looking forward to the meal.

With Bill off to complain about the delay, he walked outside onto the terrace in the hope of catching a passing breeze. It was hot and humid and dark outside. There were stars in the sky and a sliver of moon reflecting on the sea enhanced the evening view. He wished Janey was with him to share it and, more than anything, he wished he'd had a chance to explain things properly. He'd been distracted by her dropping the bombshell about her not being engaged any more. He couldn't have cared less about Honey sleeping with Janey's fiancé, but of course it was a big deal to Janey, so now he appreciated that he might have been a bit more sympathetic.

A few minutes later, Bill was back and he was in a panic.

'No food?' Travis asked him.

'No caterers, no nothing. They've gone. No sign of them. Unbloody unbelievable!'

They stood there looking at each other for a moment, thinking how strange that was and then they both immediately jumped to the same conclusion. They raced to Janey's room, pausing momentarily like gentleman to call her name at the closed door and banged loudly on it when there was again no response. Travis tried the door. It wasn't locked. He entered and his eyes scanned the room.

The dressing table still contained her things and her suitcase was still sitting there, so she couldn't have left on her own devices, but she was certainly gone.

They looked at each other and hardly dared to voice their fears.

The silence was broken by the telephone ringing in the sitting room.

They raced back to it. Bill answered it breathlessly, switching on the speakerphone.

The words from the other end were sinister and chilling…

'You know that we have her and you know what we'll do to her if you alert the police or anyone else. I'll call again in one hour.'

'Who are you?' Bill demanded.

Travis was afraid that he already knew; the fugitive had obviously managed to round up some accomplices.

Bill replaced the handset. 'No doubt they'll be calling back with their demands.'

Travis groaned and collapsed into the nearest armchair. 'This is all my fault. I was afraid of this happening but she wouldn't believe me. They must have found out she was here even though we've been so careful to keep her under the radar.'

'She went out shopping today on her own. I was worried sick.'

'Well, we already know what they'll demand. It'll be me not testifying.'

'What do we do?' Bill asked, his voice choked with panic.

'We wait for the next call and we try to find out where they have her.'

'Do you think we should involve the authorities once we have their instructions?'

'No, we can't risk it. We know what they are capable of and we must take what they've said very seriously. They will kill her if they even suspect we've gone to the police.'

To fill in some time and sate their hunger, Travis went into the kitchen and made some sandwiches from what he could find in the fridge. If they were in for a long night, which he suspected they were, then they'd need all their strength and wits about them.

They ate in silence, both struggling to find the enthusiasm to eat.

Travis was busy trying to anticipate their next move. He looked at his watch.

Bill put down what remained of his sandwich; his appetite gone.

When the phone rang he grabbed it. 'Yes?'

'If you want to see Miss Sinclair alive again then Travis Mathews will not testify in court tomorrow. Is that absolutely clear?'

'Is she okay? Where is she?' Travis demanded.

'When will she be freed?' Bill pleaded.

But whomever it was had hung up.

'He's keeping it brief in case we are tracing the call,' Travis said, fuming.

'And that's what we should be doing, isn't it?'

'Nah, waste of time. It'll be a burn phone and they'll be mobile. What we need to do is find out where they are keeping Janey.'

They both thought hard. Their brows furrowed with the effort.

'Where would be the best place to take her, if we were her kidnappers?' Travis wondered aloud.

'Somewhere off the island?' Booty suggested to him with a shrug.

They both then came to the same conclusion. 'The blow hole!'

'It would make sense. They would certainly want me off looking for her while the court is in session tomorrow,' Travis concluded.

Janey woke up with a hood over her head. It was tied around her neck and it was so hot and stuffy she thought she might suffocate. Terrified, she realised she was still lying on the hard floor of the van she had been bundled into sometime earlier. Her arms were tied behind her back and her muscles ached and burned. It was impossible for her to make any movement except to squirm like a worm.

*How long had she been lying here?*

A moment later, she heard the van door slide open and she was being dragged outside.

'Where are you taking me?' she shouted, as she was manhandled from the van.

'No talking!' said a man's voice. His voice was deep and he sounded scary.

Lifting her as if she were a sack of potatoes, he flung her over his shoulder and began walking with her. His body was big and hard and strong, and his stride was long. When he put her down onto her feet again, she realised from the sway that she was on the deck of a boat.

She was pushed down into a corner of what had to be the wheelhouse.

She could smell diesel in the air as the boat's engine fired up.

She sat quietly, trying to calm herself and compose her thoughts.

She felt a bit foolish now. Travis had warned her she was a target for the pirates and she hadn't believed him. He'd also said that if she hadn't left Antigua for the UK when she did, she would have been offered personal protection by the police and that's why he had dismissed her so cruelly, to make her leave. He *had* been telling the truth, after all.

So she guessed she was now being held to blackmail Travis into not testifying. Without Travis attending court tomorrow, the pirate killer would undoubtedly walk away from a murder charge. She just hoped Travis had the good sense to do the right thing and make sure that he made it into court. In the meantime, she had to stay focussed on staying alive until the trial was over and he came looking for her. *Surely he and Bill would come looking?*

After what had to be a few hours, they must have reached their destination because Janey's hood was removed. She gulped the fresh sea air into her lungs. In the heat of the hood, breathing in her own carbon dioxide and the diesel fumes had made her feel doubly queasy.

She couldn't focus her eyes at first. Then she saw them: two big and burly men.

They were strangers to her but they both had the same tribal neck tattoo that she recognised from the pirate gang in custody.

*Where were they taking her?*

*Was it somewhere where Travis would never find her?*

*Or were they simply taking her out to sea to throw her overboard and be rid of her?*

Tears of fear welled in her eyes. She blinked them quickly away.

'What are you going to do with me?' she asked the one steering the boat. She recognised him as the one in the catering outfit with the tray of canapés at Bill's villa. So that's how they'd bypassed the security system. Her voice was quiet and sounded much calmer than she actually felt.

The man scowled at her but he didn't answer.

Help will come, she told herself silently over and over again.

*Think only positive thoughts.*

She wondered what time it might be and looked up at the night sky to find the North Star. It shone down on her through the misted-up window of the wheelhouse and there too was the moon. A tiny slice of moon, just as it had been the last time she'd seen it from Booty's veranda.

It was around two am on the same night.

'Water, please?' she asked the man.

He threw his water bottle at her and it landed on her legs. She had no way of opening it with her arms restrained behind her and he didn't offer to help her. Instead, he brought the boat to a full stop and went to assist the other man, who was weighing anchor.

Janey stared at the bottle of water and imagined drinking it.

Soon she was dragged to her feet again. She pleaded with them to untie her hands and to let her drink water. To her surprise, they did as she asked this time. Then they tied her hands again but in front of her body this time. The relief on her screaming shoulder muscles and her dry throat was incredible. She found herself actually thanking them.

Then, gathering her wits together, she realised exactly where she was and she groaned as she saw the two voluptuous peaks soaring into the sky above her. She was truly sick of this place now. She felt she'd had enough vacation and enough adventure to last her a lifetime. She just wanted to go home to Scotland.

Once they were ashore, they marched her across the beach and hauled her up a rocky slope.

The other man kept a tight grip on Janey's arm. She had to run to keep up with his long strides. She'd realised what was going to happen to her long before they reached the gaping hole beneath their feet on the top the headland.

*They were going to throw her into the blow hole!*

'Our boss says you are to suffer the same fate that you and your meddling friends had planned for him,' said the man tightly gripping her arm.

'Oh, goody, then I can expect the coastguard to come along and rescue me in about half an hour, can I? she replied snarkily.

'Jump!' the man shouted to her, indicating to the black hole.

'No, please... I can't!' she yelled. She knew there was a deep pool of water below to break her fall but it was an awful long way down and it was too dark for her to see. She was absolutely terrified. The other man shone his torch into the hole and he winced. He must have felt sorry for her then, because he told her to wait, that he'd go and get a rope from the boat.

'Boss didn't say to kill you, so we'll lower you down.'

She thanked him profusely. As he made his way back down the hill, she smiled at the man left guarding her. 'It's a lovely moon tonight, isn't it,' she said, pointing up.

The moment the man looked up at the moon, she made a dash along the headland in the direction of the jungle. She thought she might be able to hide there until help came. She ran as fast as she could in her bare feet but, unfortunately, it was not quite as fast as the man catching up with her.

He grabbed her by the hair and Janey felt herself being hauled into the air.

She screamed loudly as he dragged her back to the blow hole, and then even louder as he picked her up and threw her straight into it.


It was just before midnight. Travis had calculated that if they left immediately, they could go straight to the blow hole, find Janey, rescue her, and be back in

Antigua in time for his court appearance at nine am. Bill sucked his breath in and shook his head; he was clearly less optimistic about the timing.

'We'll need a lot of rope and we'll need torches. Come on, Boots, we have no time to waste,' ordered Travis.

They left the marina quietly and then made good speed. It took them two and a half hours to reach the island. They cruised towards it stealthily and without lights so they could maintain the element of surprise if they needed it. He just hoped they weren't falling straight into a trap.

Ashore, they stayed out of sight, using the cover of rocks and trees to move from the beach to the headland. They communicated with each other in the dark grey light using diver signals.

When they reached the headland they moved carefully. Judging distance in the dark was difficult but once they found the blow hole, they shone a bright torch into it and called out Janey's name.

'Is that you, Bill?' she yelled back. Her voice sounded like a distant echo.

'Janey, where are the men who took you? Are they still around?' yelled Travis.

'No, I don't think so, although I can't be sure. I haven't seen them for a few hours.'

'Are you okay? Are you hurt?' Bill asked her.

'I'm cold and wet and I can't see anything. I don't have a torch.'

'We have ropes. I'm gonna come down there and get you out,' Travis assured her.

He and Bill worked to secure the rope and then Travis carefully dropped down into the hole.

He wore a head torch while Booty shone the large torch light onto him as he progressed towards Janey. Once he had her in his arms, Travis bound her to him with a quickly fashioned rope harness and began the climb back up. The climb was slow and difficult. Janey pressed herself tightly to his body, feeling the warmth of him as he made his way back up the rope. He stopped at a point about half way up to rest for a moment and to adjust his grip on the knots he had tied to aid his climb. In that time, while as they swung together on the rope, he looked into her eyes and quickly kissed her on the lips.

At the top of the hole, Bill helped them both onto a secure footing. He took the harness off Janey and he hugged her. She hugged him back in relief. She was cold and wet and shivering.

Bill took off his shirt and draped it over her trembling shoulders. 'Take off your wet dress if you can, Janey.'

She slipped her dress off from under the cover of his shirt and felt his residual body heat warm her. When Travis did the same for her, she was doubly warm.

'I knew you'd find me. I knew you'd come. I just didn't expect it to be until tomorrow,' she told them. 'I expected you to stay on Antigua, Travis, until after the trial. You do know you have to be in court in exactly three hours time, don't you?'

He looked at her in dismay. He was being told off again for rescuing her.

'Can't you just be a little bit grateful?' he said in exasperation.

'I just don't want the pirate killer to be freed just because you played right into their hands and came all the way out here looking for me, that's all.'

*There was absolutely no winning with her.*

They got back on board the *Salva Vida* and raced back to Antigua. As they pulled into the marina, Janey gave them back their shirts so they wouldn't have to go into court half naked, and slipped back into her cocktail dress that she'd had blowing in the warm breeze all the way back.

The three of them raced along the dock, hailed a taxi and arrived at the court house with a whole ten minutes to spare.

When the pirate killer took his place in the dock, to say he was surprised to see Travis and Janey in court was an understatement. He kept blinking at them as if he was only imagining them there.

The trial lasted exactly four hours and the jury deliberated their verdict for just thirty minutes.

The accused was found guilty on twenty counts of piracy, several counts of kidnapping and extortion, and the verdict that everyone held their breath on as it was read out by the jury spokesperson.

'Murder in the first degree... guilty.'

The judge thanked the jury for their public duty and for their sound verdict. She also made a point of thanking Travis for his testimony.

When the gavel went down and the court was dismissed, the pirate killer was led back to jail to serve several life sentences.

Janey looked at Travis and Bill. They looked exhausted and dishevelled in an overdressed sort of way, but they were hugging each other like brothers again.

# Chapter Twenty

Her bag was packed. All that remained now was to say thank you and goodbye to Bill. He'd been so good to her and she would miss him. She opened the bedroom door and walked straight into Travis. She stared at him uneasily and wondered what to say to him.

'Sorry, Janey. I was just about to knock. Can we talk?'

She hesitated and realising he didn't mean in the hallway, she took a step back into the room.

He saw her suitcase on the bed. 'You're leaving?'

'Yes, I am.'

He reached for her hand. 'Janey, you can't go. I want you to stay.'

She shook him off. 'No, please, don't. This is embarrassing enough for me as it is. You know I came back here on the pretence of claiming a share of the treasure, but it was never about the coins, Travis. I fell in love with you when we were on that island together and I came back to find out for sure if I had a chance with you. But don't worry, you have made it quite clear once again how you feel.'

'That's not true. I do love you. Why don't you believe me?'

'I think you know why, and it's not because you spent the whole of the past week trying to suggest that I leave. It was because you slept with Honey.'

'Janey, I really need to explain something to you, and you need to listen to me this time. Honey might have slept in my bed, but that night I slept on the sofa. The next morning I made it very clear to her that she had to get herself a room somewhere else.'

'Really?'

*Should she believe him? Oh boy did she want to believe him – and as it turned out he hadn't been lying to her all week after all. He had actually been telling the truth about her being in mortal danger.*

'Yes. Really. Nothing happened. In fact, I think you owe me an apology.'

'Ha! You think? Maybe it's that we just got off on the wrong foot again. Perhaps we should start over. Okay, how about we both make an effort this time?' she said to him.

He raised his chin in a way that suggested he might actually be up for the idea.

Then he whipped his good arm around her waist and pulled her tightly against him.

'You want us to start over and pretend that I'm not a grumpy old sea captain and you're not a tourist?'

'I think we could make it work.'

She heard herself moan with joy as his lips came crashing down on hers.

It was the kiss she'd been dreaming of ever since he had first kissed her at the top of the waterfall. She wrapped her arms around his neck and was about lose control of her sensibilities, when she realised exactly where they were.

'Not here,' she said to him softly. 'We can't possibly make love in Bill's guest room.' She indicated towards her suitcase. 'We need to go somewhere a little more private.'

He sighed and his eyes shone at her playfully. 'Arh, so now you're willing to come and stay at my beach house?'

'Well... Of course, I'd have to see it first.'

'Then it's probably only fair to warn you, it's more of a beach shack, really.'

## A week or so later…

At the far side of the marina, at dry dock, repair works had begun in earnest on *The Mermaid*. There wasn't a cloud in the sky or a whiff of sea breeze in the hot humid air as Janey, Travis and Booty Bill took a break from restoring the damaged wheelhouse to sit on three upturned buckets on the partly charred deck.

'Well, here we are again,' Janey quipped. 'I have to say that joining a United Nations debate on world affairs might be easier than trying to reach a definitive agreement with you two.'

'Yeah, come on. It's high time we made a decision once and for all on what we do with the coins,' said Travis, ramming his sunglasses onto his face. 'I'm in favour of getting wet, getting rich and keeping things very much under the radar. I've a boat to rebuild and a roof to fix.'

'Perhaps we should take a democratic vote. Two against one wins?' she suggested.

Bill immediately disagreed. 'No. I'm on board *only* if we do this by the Code.'

Travis shrugged and then slapped his hands down onto his bare knees. 'Here we go again. Okay, where do you stand, Janey? Are you with Boots or with me?'

She hesitated for a second, thus betraying to Travis where her loyalties might lie.

Travis stood up and began pacing the deck in frustration.

Janey quickly continued. 'Look, I have an idea that I want you to at least consider. We all know it's going to be practically impossible to dispose of these coins unless we sell just a few at a time and, unless we do things by the Code, we risk going to jail.'

'So what do you propose?' Travis asked.

'I propose we leave the coins exactly where they are and we tell no one they even exist.'

Travis hooted with laughter. 'What? That's crazy! We just forget about them?'

'No. But we keep them secret and in doing so, we become the guardians of the legend.'

Bill made a grunting noise the way he did when he was amused.

Janey looked at Travis. 'What do you think of that idea, Captain Mathews?'

Travis raised his chin. 'Mmm… I quite like the idea of being a guardian of the legend.'

Then she turned to Bill. 'What's funny, Boots?'

'What's funny is listening to you two babbling over these coins all day and every day like they were they only coins to ever go missing in the whole of the Caribbean.'

Janey and Travis looked at each other, both wondering what exactly he meant by that statement.

Booty continued. 'Did you know that maybe as many as four *thousand* ships have sunk in the Caribbean over the years? And yet you could hunt the sea for your whole life and never find one of them. That's because the tides and shifting sands can cover a ship or move the wreckage miles and miles away from its original site.'

Janey listened to him, totally mesmerised. She loved it when Booty talked treasure.

Suddenly he flipped something into the air and she caught it. She studied it for a moment before saying, 'It's a coin dated 1755, and I think it might be Dutch.'

'Yes, you're right. I believe it to be part of a Dutch East India Company cargo that was lost off the tiny volcanic island of Saba in 1756. *The Van Kreuning* was the largest ship in the Dutch fleet. Its manifest showed that she was carrying over a thousand pounds of gold bullion packed into seventeen chests, over fifteen thousand gold doubloons, more than one million pieces of eight, seven hundred ounces of silver, and several chests of precious stones. It's all still missing to this day.'

Janey passed the coin to Travis, whose jaw had just dropped. 'And this *is* a gold doubloon, if I'm not mistaken,' he spluttered.

'Yep, minted the year before the loss of *The Van Kreuning*. Could be a coincidence, of course.'

Janey and Travis were suddenly back sitting on their upturned buckets enthralled by this tale from the shipwreck master himself.

'How did you find it, Booty?'

'Quite by accident. On a beautiful day such as this, on what was an uncharted part of the reef. I came across this coin just sitting there amongst the coral at a depth of about twenty metres.'

Janey gasped in excitement. 'And you think that all the treasure from *The Van Kreuning* is still down there?'

Travis shook his head as if there was something he just couldn't process. 'Boots, can I ask why, when you've probably had this coin a while and it sounds like it could be part of a serious haul of treasure, are you showing it to us now?'

'Because it *is* a serious piece of treasure booty. Actually, I found it only a few weeks ago. I've been hesitant to tell you two treasure hunters about it until you both came to the right conclusion about the coins you found in the cave. In this case, leaving those coins exactly where they are *is* the right thing to do, but for some reason it has taken you all this time to realise it. It's not just about selling treasure and getting rich. It's about respecting history and the Code.'

Travis, clearly feeling a little humbled while he thought about this, wore a serious expression.

'I have a question,' Janey said, tentatively. 'According to the Code, who would claim legal ownership of the treasure from *The Van Kreuning*, should it ever be found?'

'That would be the government of the Netherlands, whom I've always found to be very amicable, generous and appreciative in my experiences with them concerning treasure salvage, especially when it comes to rewarding those who have returned their lost property.'

Booty stood up and stretched his legs. 'Now, if you two want to accompany me on my next vacation, I'll be setting off for the waters off Saba on the high tide tomorrow morning.'

Travis and Janey looked at each other in wide-eyed excitement.

'What do you say, are you up for another Caribbean vacation?' asked Travis.

Janey shook her head. 'No way! But if you'll call it a Caribbean adventure instead – then I'm in!'

*The End*

**BONUS CONTENT**

Turn the page to read the Prologue and Chapter One of:

**Island in the Sun by Janice Horton**

# Island in the Sun

## *Prologue*

*A small group of people are gathered on the side of a hill. The church behind them is painted white in colonial style and has a tall spire pointing into a cloudless blue sky. There is a balmy breeze blowing in from the east, whipping up the minister's white outer cassock, and causing the petals of the more delicate tropical flowers on the funeral casket to rise up and flutter about like fragrant butterflies.*

*The mourners have their heads lowered in prayer. Beneath their wide brimmed hats, their shaded eyes are firmly closed, yet the view from this lofty vantage point is stunning; a sparkling blue-green sea for a full three hundred and sixty degrees around, and below, a white-sand palm-fringed beach is shimmering in the mid-morning heat. A mound of freshly dug earth is piled neatly to one side of the grave. As the casket of their beloved matriarch Katherine Rocha is lowered into the ground some of those gathered, like her loyal housekeeper and friend Grace, are now openly weeping.*

*With a final farewell, Grace wipes away her tears and takes solace in remembering the good times, when Miss Kate had first arrived on this laid-back little island in the Caribbean Sea with her handsome husband Mr Ernest Rocha, and their sophisticated glamour and pizzazz. When they had taken on an army of workers from the village to fix up the old owner's house and even put in a tennis court and a swimming pool and how everyone, from fisherman to fisherwife, had wanted to work for the rich and fabulous new owners of Pearl Island.*

*When Miss Kate had let it be known that she was looking for a cook and a housekeeper, Grace had proudly secured both positions and some of her favourite memories were of cooking for the Rocha's and their friends and visitors from America who had come over to stay on the island at one time or another. On these occasions, she would prepare elaborate dinners while Mr Ernest, dressed to the nines in his dapper style, served aperitifs on the porch and Miss Kate looked the belle of the ball in the latest chic designer gowns and fabulous jewellery. In those halcyon days, in the kitchen below the porch, Grace would sway her hips to the music wafting in through the open windows with the smoke from Mr Ernest's Cuban cigars and the lively conversation, laughter, and heady perfume.*

*Grace sighed. Those were the days before Mr Ernest was missing, his body never recovered. The days before poor Miss Kate was left bereft and grieving. The days before salvation came to the island in the form of Miss Kate's little orphaned niece. Tears welled up once more in Grace's eyes as she remembered her great affection for Isla.*

*Isla – a name that means island – came to live on Pearl Island as a six-year-old after the death of her own parents in England. With her sweetheart-shaped face and her white blonde hair and bright blue eyes, Isla had grown up a happy and carefree island child, bringing joy and laughter to a deathly-quiet house and a heartbroken Miss Kate back from the brink of her terrible grief.*

*But just a decade later, heartbreak had returned, when at sixteen-years-old, a rebellious and devilishly headstrong Isla, made the mistake of falling in love with Leo Fernandez, the son of notorious islander Jack Fernandez. She had been warned off seeing the sea-gypsy boy by her anxious aunt but Isla had steadfastly refused to listen and just as her aunt predicted and feared, a terrible incident led to eighteen-year-old Leo being arrested and Isla being despatched by her angry Aunt to a boarding school in the UK.*

*Since that day, Miss Kate had refused to mention the girl's name. However, a photograph of Isla, taken on her sixteenth birthday, has remained on Miss Kate's bedside table to this very day. Now that Miss Kate was no longer here, Grace could only pray that what happened a decade ago, although serious enough to break her employer's heart, had not given enough cause for Miss Kate to ever remove her niece, her only surviving relative, from her last Will and Testament and that Isla could return to Pearl Island to claim what was rightfully hers.*

# Island in the Sun
# Chapter One
*Isla – Present Day*

Isla hauled her suitcase up the path to her front door and noticed a dark-coloured car parked on the opposite side of the street. There was a man inside it and he was quite obviously watching her. Did she know him? No, she didn't think so, because she didn't know anyone in Edinburgh who drove a Bentley.

Her pace quickened while her hand searched inside her jacket pocket for her key. What was he doing there? What did he want? In alarm, she wondered if burglars or people-traffickers, even rapists, were using expensive cars these days as some kind of decoy for their evil intentions. If so, then luckily she wasn't easily fooled nor impressed.

From across the street she heard the car door click open and then clunk heavily shut. She gripped the key in her hand and readied it to use as a weapon should she need to defend herself, although she doubted she had the energy for a fight. It had been a long day, her flight had been delayed, and she just wanted to come home to a hot bath and a glass of wine.

Then she heard the man call out her name.

'Isla Ashton?' He used a tone of inflection, as if not actually calling her name but asking if it was her name.

She turned on her heels to see him walking towards her. She quickly noticed he was smartly dressed and looked more like a private detective than an assailant.

'Who are you?' she demanded.

'My name is Mark King. My legal office in Edinburgh has been charged with the task of informing you of the recent death of your aunt, Mrs Katherine Rocha.'

*Auntie Kate was dead?*

At the news, Isla wavered on her feet.

Mark King, reaching out to her with his business card, caught her arm.

'I'm really sorry, Miss Ashton. I can see this has come as something of a shock. Perhaps we should discuss this matter inside?' He motioned towards the front door of her town house.

Isla glanced over his card to note his name was embossed in gold lettering. She nodded as her throat felt too tight to speak and she attempted to open the door with a trembling hand. On her third attempt, Mark King offered to help. She handed over the key to him and he rattled it in the lock for a fraction of a second before pushing open the door. It was then she noticed that he was carrying something tucked under his arm, a parcel, wrapped in brown paper and tied up with string.

He stood aside and she slid past him. Flicking on the hallway light, Isla looked around her.

'Sorry about the mess,' she said, and scooped up five days of post from the floor and rushed to clear magazines from the sofa so that he could sit down. But he was already in her kitchen, filling the kettle from the tap.

While sipping tea, Mark King told her that her aunt had died of cancer. 'Diagnosed two years ago, apparently, but she refused treatment.'

Isla sighed. 'I guess she wouldn't leave the island.'

'I couldn't find a private number for you,' he explained apologetically. 'But I did leave messages at the number listed on your company website and I also sent an email. I'm sorry, but it has been a little difficult to track you down, Miss Ashton.'

'I've been away on business and I gave my PA some time off. When is the funeral?'

Mark King looked even more uncomfortable as he told her, 'It is today. On the island.' He retrieved the parcel he had been carrying and placed it on the coffee table in front of her.

Isla stared at it. 'What is that?'

'Your aunt's executors in Grand Cayman understand that it belongs to you. It's not listed as part of her estate and she left specific instructions it be returned to you in the event of her death.'

She put down her tea and pulled the wrapping off the parcel. She recognised the box beneath immediately and pressed her hands to her mouth to cover the smile that had begun to play on her lips.

It was Aunt Kate's jewellery box.

Isla was suddenly struck with some of her happiest memories. Sneaking barefoot across the painted wooden porch into her aunt's bedroom through doors left open to encourage a cooling breeze to blow in from the sea, to dance around in her aunt's colourful batik sarongs.

In her mind's eye, she saw an ethereal image of herself as a small girl, draped in those wonderfully light gossamer fabrics, sitting at her aunt's dressing table and playing dress-up with her vast collection of rubies and emeralds and diamonds and pearls.

She also tried to hide her surprise that her aunt would have actually wanted her to have her jewellery after what had happened although, of course, it made perfect sense that she wouldn't have wanted it all in the hands of the taxman or her lawyers.

Her aunt's jewellery would be worth an absolute fortune. Not that there had ever been any record of its worth or even its existence. It had never been valued or insured and there were certainly no receipts because none of it had ever actually been purchased. The pearls – perfectly formed and natural – had mostly been found a long time ago off the very island that Isla had once called home. The diamonds and other precious stones in the collection had without a doubt been either won or hustled by Isla's infamous late Uncle Ernest Rocha, at high-stakes poker games during the 1970s, which is exactly how he had come to own a whole Caribbean island in the first place.

'Yes, it came to me through my late parents and has been in the safekeeping of my aunt,' Isla lied.

Lying came surprisingly easy to her, probably because she herself had been lied to so convincingly.

Mark King nodded and seemed satisfied.

Isla allowed her fingers to reach out and wander over the familiar shimmering mother-of-pearl mosaic of starfish and seahorses and shells that decorated the box. It was beautiful. Just as beautiful as she remembered it.

'Although, there doesn't appear to be a key,' Mark King pointed out.

Isla raised an eyebrow. She recalled a cleverly hidden compartment that held a key beneath the beautifully carved façade. She stood up, offering him her hand for shaking, now that their business was concluded. 'Thank you, Mr King. I appreciate you coming out here to deliver this box to me personally.'

He took an envelope from the inside pocket of his jacket. 'Your aunt's Last Will and Testament will be read in a few days' time and as per her wishes you are required to attend.' He placed the envelope straight into her hand. 'This is a first-class air ticket. Your flight leaves tomorrow.'

Isla vehemently shook her head. 'No, I can't possibly. Anyway, there's little point. You see, my Aunt Kate and I had a big falling out, a long time ago, and we haven't been in contact since. I really have no interest in going back there.'

Mark King's dark eyebrows rose up and disappeared under his thatch of dark hair.

'But, Miss Ashton, I don't think you fully understand. Estranged or not, I have been advised that you are about to inherit her estate in its entirety, and by that, I mean the island in the Caribbean Sea known as *Isla de las Perlas* and all the properties and the businesses thereon. You are absolutely required to go and attend the reading. I'm afraid it's an obligation.'

***Did you enjoy reading this sample…?***

*<u>Island in the Sun</u> is available from Amazon sites worldwide both in paperback or to download to your Kindle ereader or to read on your own device using the free Amazon Kindle App.*

## About the Author

Janice Horton, also known as the backpacking housewife, writes contemporary romantic fiction with a dash of humour and a sense of adventure. Once her three children had grown up, Janice and her backpacking husband sold their empty nest in Scotland UK along with almost everything they owned and set off to travel the world. Since then they have been travelling full-time and have explored over 50 countries, living out of an apartment, a hut, or wherever they happen to find themselves.

Janice works as a writer wherever she is in the world. Look out for her 'Backpacking Housewife' series of novels published by HarperCollins and her bestselling backlist of romantic adventure novels. When not writing novels, she writes lifestyle and travel features for her website at 'The Backpacking Housewife Dotcom' and her work has also featured in national and international magazines like 'Prima' and 'Bella' in the UK and 'Friday' in Dubai. Janice has also been involved in BBC Scotland's Write Here Write Now project and has been interviewed on many travel podcasts and radio shows including Loose Women's Kaye Adams' prime time BBC Radio Scotland Show.

*Click HERE to see Janice Horton's Book List on Amazon*

**Follow Janice Horton on Social Media**

**Website:** https://thebackpackinghousewife.com/

**HarperCollins:**
https://www.harpercollins.co.uk/author/cr-120947/janice-horton/

**Instagram:**
https://www.instagram.com/janicehortonwriter/

**Twitter:** https://twitter.com/JaniceHorton

**Facebook**:
https://www.facebook.com/TheBackpackingHousewife/

**Pinterest:**
https://www.pinterest.co.uk/TheBackpackingHousewife/

Printed in Great Britain
by Amazon